THE TASTE OF ROMANCE

ARCADIA VALLEY ROMANCE BOOK 18 / LEGACY OF
THE HEART BOOK 3

DANICA FAVORITE

For all the mothers, trying to do the best they can for their children.

CHAPTER 1

*S*o this was Bigby Farm. Madison McKay pulled into
the driveway and took in the buildings around her.
To her left was a sprawling yellow farmhouse with random-
looking, tacked on bits that must have been added over the
years. Straight ahead were a series of barns and a large
parking lot. And to the right was a large field of narrow,
purple flowers that looked like lavender. Though they'd
passed many farms along the way that reeked of manure, this
place smelled fresh, clean. A far cry from the ramshackle
dump her mother used to complain about. Actually, to hear
her mother speak of Bigby Farm, one would think it was one
of the levels of hell as described in Dante's Inferno. Which
ring depended upon how charitable her mother was feeling
toward her in-laws.

Madison didn't have very many memories of the Bigby
side of the family. Her dad had died when she was young,
and her mother had cut off all contact, blaming the Bigbys
for her husband's death and saying they would ruin Madison's life. They hadn't. Madison had done a fine job of
ruining her life all on her own. Which was why she found

herself walking up the steps of the front porch with her three children. D.J., Faith, and two-year-old Hope, the bonus baby everyone thought would make things better, but had marked the beginning of the end for her marriage. Not that it was Hope's fault. In many ways, Madison was grateful for the tiny little girl who'd given her the strength to do the right thing when she'd lost her ability to see straight.

Which is why it didn't seem so crazy that she'd accepted a long-lost cousin's invitation to stay with their grandmother while she figured out how to get back on her feet after her husband ran off to an ashram in India with his yoga instructor. The kind of thing she thought only happened in movies, but now, it was real life. The problem with spending her entire adult life as a stay-at-home mom was that when her husband took all the money, leaving her with nothing but debt and three children who didn't stop growing simply because she couldn't afford to buy them new clothes, she didn't have a lot of options.

She knocked on the front door, but was met with silence. She'd told them to expect her around four, and it was five until. Maybe they were running late, and she was just a tad bit early.

"What is this place?" D. J. asked, looking around. "Is this where Dad is?"

Every single day. She had to answer the exact same question. Where was their father? Neither she nor the kids had heard from him in nearly six months. It must have felt even longer to the kids, who didn't understand why their father was on a quest to find himself. Dave McKay, from the outside, was the picture-perfect example of what a father should be. At least until the morning he didn't return from his business trip, and instead sent her an email, telling her he needed time to figure out who he was.

As many times as she'd read that email, and the few that

had come since, Madison still didn't understand. So how could she get her children to?

"No. I told you," she explained. Again. "We're going to stay with my grandmother and my cousins for a while. Won't it be fun to have family around us?"

One more thing the children had no concept of. Both Madison and Dave had been only children, and Dave's parents were long gone. Madison's mother was also an only child, and the lack of connection to the Bigbys, until now, had meant that they didn't have many family connections. When they'd first gotten together, Madison and Dave had talked about having a large family. D.J.'s early arrival and rushed wedding was supposed to be the start of their dreams coming true. But after Faith, Dave's career took off, and he thought everything was just perfect. All the people he tried to impress had a similarly perfect family with a son, a daughter, and a trophy wife. Little did those perfect people know, all it took to fall from the pedestal was another unplanned pregnancy and subsequent weight gain that was a lot harder to bounce back from at thirty than it had been at twenty. At least, that's what Madison assumed had been the problem, based on all of Dave's fat jokes.

The kids hadn't answered Madison's question, but she hadn't expected them to. They wore the same shell-shocked expression that hadn't left their faces since she'd told them their father wasn't coming home. How could it make sense to them, when everything had seemed fine prior to Dave's leaving? It wasn't until the bill collectors started calling and Madison started digging into their finances that she realized her husband had been leading a double life for years.

Fabulous for Dave, that he could find a way to start all over in creating his dream life. And goody for him that after years of feeling like he'd lost himself, he could now find the path to enlightenment. She just wished he'd had the guts to explain it to his kids.

She took Hope's hand. "Why don't we walk around and take a look at the farm while we wait?"

"Maybe we can find a place with Wi-Fi," D.J. said, the usual irritation lining his voice.

She'd had to give up their cell plan a few months ago, when the money had run out. No, not money. Their credit limit. What had Dave been thinking, buying the kids expensive cell phones just before he left and not leaving Madison a way to pay for it? Everyone thought she just hadn't tried hard enough or was sitting around, doing nothing all day. But she had literally never held a job. As a teenager, her mother hadn't let her work, wanting her to focus on her studies. The same for college. Since she'd left school a semester before graduation to have D. J., she'd been a stay-at-home mom. Any time she'd talked about going back to school and finishing her degree or even finding a job, so she could do something with herself while the kids were in school, Dave had gotten angry and asked her why the life he'd given her wasn't enough.

Though she'd never been one for violence, sometimes she wanted to punch him in the nose for that one. He'd left her completely alone with no options for survival because his life wasn't enough, but she was supposed to have been satisfied with the way he had left her helpless.

"I'm hungry," Faith said.

They'd passed a fast food place about an hour ago, and even though the kids begged to stop, Madison had pressed on, eager to get here, but also painfully aware that she had less than $100 to her name and she wasn't sure how long she would need it to stretch. She'd been ashamed to explain her financial situation to her grandmother and cousin Allie, especially since her mother had said she'd brought it on herself. Her mother was another person who didn't understand why Dave had left. The perfect husband didn't suddenly decide he hated his life, so surely Madison had done something wrong.

Well, she could admit to a lot of things, but mostly she'd been wrong in blindly trusting him and thinking they were happy. She'd thought that that's what you're supposed to do in a marriage, and had Dave given her any indication that he wanted things to be different, she would have done her best to change. But other than going on more diets to combat his snide comments about her weight, and visiting a counselor he refused to see, she hadn't known what else to do.

Fortunately, before Madison could patiently explain once again that they still had some carrots to snack on in the car, a man came around the side of the house.

All three children huddled closer to her, and as Madison looked at the man, she couldn't help putting her arms around them. If they weren't on the farm in the middle of nowhere, she would have thought he was a homeless man. His hair was long and shaggy, and his beard wasn't the neatly kept hipster style of the men they knew back home, even though he couldn't have been much older than them. He wore baggy, dirty jeans, and a T-shirt that looked like it belonged in the rag pile as opposed to on a man's body. His hands and arms were covered in dirt all the way up to his elbows. Mud caked his clothing.

"If you're here to sell Enid something, she's not interested. Nice touch bringing the kids though." Then he paused. "It's not cookie season, is it? School's out for the year, but..."

She opened her mouth to explain who she was, but didn't get the chance.

He looked them up and down. "Oh, wait. I forgot the youth group is doing a fundraiser for camp. I'm sorry. I should have guessed that with you bringing the kids, that was the case. You must be the new family to town. Sorry we haven't had a chance to meet, but I've been gone the past couple of weeks.

"Wade Ellis." He held out his filthy hand.

Madison must've given him a funny look, because he looked down at it, then groaned.

"Sorry about that," he said, brushing his hand on his equally filthy pants. "I've been transplanting lavender for Allie all day, and I didn't pay much attention to my appearance coming out to see who was on Enid's front porch."

At least now, things were starting to make sense. Her cousin Allie used Bigby Farm to run a lavender operation. She grew lavender and made all kinds of products out of it that she sold at various farmers' markets and regional boutiques. This man must be a migrant worker she hired during her busy season.

"I hope I didn't offend you too much with my comments about you guys trying to sell us something. A lot of people want to take advantage of an old woman living alone, and I get a little protective. Still, I'm always happy to support the youth group." He reached into his back pocket and pulled out a wallet. "What fundraiser did they decide on? None of the other kids have hit me up yet, but I'm always happy to donate to everyone."

Was it weird to like someone so immediately? The guy might be a migrant worker, but to be willing to donate to every kid going to camp was pretty special. He reminded her of Mrs. Sanders, who lived down the block from her growing up. Even though the old widow had no money, any time any of the kids came by with a school fundraiser, she always pressed a quarter into their hands, telling them it wasn't much, but she hoped it would help. People like this Wade guy and Mrs. Sanders always made her feel ashamed for how she and Dave used to live. They'd had plenty of money—at least, until Dave ran out on them—and while they gave their requisite tithes to the church, it certainly wasn't the kind of sacrificial giving she saw here.

She smiled at him. "Thank you, but we're not here for a donation. I'm Madison McKay, Enid's granddaughter, and we're here for a visit."

Wade's eyes widened. "Allie said you weren't coming until the fifth."

"Today is the fifth." She tried not to sound rude in her answer, especially because this guy was trying to be helpful.

He shook his head, looking disgusted. "I'm so sorry. I should pay better attention to the calendar. Allie is going to kill me when she finds out." Then he grinned. "But she'll get over it as soon as she meets you. I don't know who was more excited, Allie or Enid. I guess I don't need to tell you how much Allie has enjoyed emailing with you."

This man sounded much more familiar with the family's inner workings than a seasonal migrant worker. But as Madison mentally went through the list of family members she remembered Allie discussing with her, she couldn't recall hearing about a Wade.

"I'm looking forward to it," Madison said. "We're just waiting for them to get home."

Wade laughed. "Oh, they're home, all right. Enid was baking up a storm this morning. I'm sure they're in the kitchen waiting for you. No one uses the front door, which is why I thought you were a salesperson. Come on. Let's go say hi to everyone."

It would have been nice for Allie to warn her that no one used the front door, but as they walked around the back of the house, and she saw all the cars parked there, it would have been clear to Madison that's where she should have gone.

Before they got halfway down the walk, the door opened,

and an older woman, with white hair and sparkling eyes, came rushing out. Though she looked far too young to be in her eighties, Madison knew that this was her grandmother.

A strange sense of peace filled her as Enid wrapped her arms around Madison, and the older woman whispered, "Thank you God, for answering my prayers."

Madison had gone to church her whole life, and she had never experienced such a genuine confession of gratitude as she did now. Funny, considering she saw Enid as an answer to her prayers, rather than the other way around. And yet, as she remembered Wade's words about people wanting to take advantage of an older woman, she felt slightly guilty. Though it was true Enid was offering her a place to stay to get back on her feet, Madison was also grateful to reconnect with the side of the family she didn't know. Hopefully, no one would think that the only reason she was here was for money.

She squeezed her grandmother tight. "And thank you for being an answer to mine."

Enid pulled away. "None of that. We're family. This is what family is for. Now let me meet those great-grandchildren of mine. Since everyone else around here is being stubborn about giving me some, at least now I have some youngsters to enjoy."

Madison nudged her son. "This is David Junior, but we all call him D.J. He's eleven, and he loves computer games."

She had to sell his game console a couple of months ago to help pay the electric bill. He still hadn't forgiven her, but she'd already sold everything else of value she had. At least that was one thing Dave had done right. Every holiday, he'd given her some expensive piece of jewelry or some other useless bauble that she hadn't much liked, but she'd dutifully accepted. Those had been easy to sell off. Her final act of desperation to get here had been hiring an estate sale company to liquidate everything else they had in her home, which hadn't been much since there weren't many valuables left. Now, all they had left was what she'd been able to fit in her car.

"Those things will rot your brain," her grandmother said.

D.J. scowled. "You don't know anything. My dad says I'm going to be a computer programmer someday and make a gazillion dollars."

Would Dave have left it he'd known just how much his son looked up to him?

Ignoring the temptation to argue with her son, Madison nudged Faith. "This is Faith. She's nine, and she loves animals. I think it's going to be great for her, living on a farm, where she can interact with them."

"My dad says farm animals are dirty and carry disease," Faith said, looking smugly at her brother. Before Dave left, Faith had always argued with her father on this point. But now, the kids seemed to desperately cling to everything he'd ever said as if they thought it would somehow bring him back.

If only.

It wasn't that Madison wanted Dave back. After everything he'd put her through, leaving her alone to figure out how to take care of her family while he found himself, she wasn't sure how she would ever be able to trust him again. Besides, the yoga instructor wasn't the first affair. It was just the first she'd found out about until she'd started going through his records.

Wade stepped forward. "They definitely can, which is why we take a lot of precautions for cleanliness here. Once you get settled in, I'll be happy to demonstrate."

Was he joking? Caked in dirt, the man was hardly the poster child for hygiene.

"You don't look like you've had a bath in months," Faith

said. "How do I know we're not going to get a disease from you?"

She hadn't raised her children to speak to adults like that and it made her heart hurt to see the disgust on her daughter's face.

"Faith! That was rude. Apologize to this nice man right now. He's just trying to help."

"Our father said homeless people are a scourge on the earth and deserve everything they get," Faith continued, ignoring Madison's request completely. "Maybe, if they made better choices, they would have better lives."

She'd never been ashamed of her children before. But the smug expressions on their faces made Madison want to cry. She'd had enough of protecting the man who'd turned such sweet human beings into monsters.

"Then take a look in the mirror," Madison said. "Because technically, you're homeless. So you get back to me on how to make better choices for your own life."

Tears filled Faith's eyes, and Madison regretted her harsh words. D.J., however, turned and glared at Madison. "You were the one who made bad choices. You made our dad leave. And maybe if you weren't lazy and got a job, we would still have all our stuff."

Dozens of people had said the same thing to Madison, including her own mother. Which was why Madison was here, dependent on the kindness of relatives she'd never even met. Everyone thought that Madison had to have done something wrong to make her husband leave the way he did. No one understood why she didn't just get a job that miraculously made everything all better. But given that they'd gone from Dave's six-figure salary to nothing and the best Madison was qualified for was flipping burgers at a local fast food place that barely paid above minimum wage, she'd be lucky if she managed to pay the utility bill, let alone the mortgage. Not that the fast food place would hire her. She'd tried.

Wade took a step toward D.J. "That's enough, young man. I might look like a homeless person to you, but I would never speak to my mother like that. I don't know you folks, and I don't know where your dad is. But if I were your dad, I'd have a good talking to you about treating people with respect. Your mother's done a good thing by bringing you here. The Bigbys are the finest people I've ever known, and I hope that a little time with them will teach you about common decency."

For a moment, everyone was silent. Madison struggled with the emotions welling up inside her. She hadn't once cried in front of her children. Not even when the man from the bank came and started taking pictures of their house to sell it out from under them. It's what happened when your husband stopped paying the mortgage months before leaving and didn't tell you. But she supposed her son was right. She'd made a bad choice in trusting that Dave was taking care of everything the way he'd said he would.

Enid cleared her throat. "It's all right, Wade. I'm sure the boy didn't mean it. It's got to be hard, losing everything the way they did, and children don't understand the ways of adults."

Tears filled the older woman's eyes, threatening to break the dam holding back the emotions Madison had been stuffing down for months. She bent and picked up Hope.

"All right then, moving on." Madison pasted a smile on her face as she gave her little girl a squeeze. "This is Hope. She's two, and an absolute delight."

"No, she's not," Faith said. "She still wets the bed."

To nine-year-olds, a bed-wetter was a terrible thing. But they had struggled with potty training, and with all the uncertainty over the past few months, it seemed more diffi-cult than ever.

Enid held out her arms. "That's all right. I've known a number of bed-wetters in my time, and I know she'll outgrow it. I've got tea that will help."

Madison had no idea how tea would help with bed-wetting, but at this point, she was willing to give it a try.

"Now that we've met everyone," Enid said. "Let's go inside and have a snack. I'm sure you're all starving after your trip."

The kids perked up at the idea of food. Wade had said Enid had been baking all day. Maybe a few tasty treats would have them warming up to the situation.

When they got into the kitchen, the spread laid out before them made Madison's heart sink. One platter had an array of fresh vegetables, including the carrots her children were starting to dread. They were an inexpensive snack, so Madison often used them to fill hungry bellies between meals. Another platter was filled with various fruits, that Madison suspected also came from the farm. She remem-bered her cousin telling her about how they preferred to use local and in season produce and grew much of their own food. Before their lives had been turned upside down, Madison prided herself on preparing only local and organic meals for her children. But as she saw the expressions on her children's faces, she realized that the children were not as impressed.

At least Enid held out a tray of freshly baked cookies to the children. They'd had to give up sweets because they'd been too expensive. The children eagerly bit into their cook-ies. Then promptly spit them out.

"Gross! What's in this?" D.J. said, making a face and sticking out his tongue.

Faith glared at Madison. "This tastes like the time you put salt instead of sugar in our muffins."

She'd only done it once, right after Dave had left, and she'd been baking to try to make herself feel better. Except when you're using the baby's nap time while the kids were at school to do so, sometimes you find yourself sobbing too hard to read the recipe properly. It was the only opportunity Madison had to cry. But children didn't understand that.

"We don't use sugar here," a woman's voice said. Madison looked up and saw her cousin Allie entering the room. "I'm sorry I wasn't here to greet you, but I had a conference call with a boutique chain interested in carrying my products and it went a little long."

Allie gave her a warm hug, and Madison was once again comforted with the feeling that she'd come home. Maybe she had made a lot of really bad decisions, but they'd all brought her here, to this place, and this moment, where she finally felt like maybe everything was going to be okay.

CHAPTER 2

*W*ade was trying not to be negative, but as excited as Enid and Allie had been that they were finally getting to know Madison and her children, it seemed like too big a challenge for them to take on. Madison seemed nice enough, but her kids were a bunch of spoiled brats, and they walked all over her. Oh, he knew the type. He'd known plenty of them in his Silicon Valley days. Madison and her kids were every bit the trophy wife and family he'd seen with all the executives he'd known. The only mystery was, where was the dad? Although the more he thought about it, the more he realized it was probably not so much of a mystery. He'd seen it too many times. Now that the dad was getting older, he probably was feeling his age, and had some pretty little secretary batting her eyes at him, telling him all the things that made him feel young and virile again, and suddenly, the wife who'd stood by him as he climbed the corporate ladder was tossed aside like the take-out cartons littering the conference room table.

It wasn't Wade's story. But that's why he'd left. He was sick and tired of watching guys throw away perfectly good lives because they bought into the lies of the world that told them they needed bigger and better to be happy. More importantly, he was tired of being judged only by the size of his bank account.

So what was Madison's deal? The luxury SUV parked outside made it seem like she came from money. Then again, most of the guys he'd known did their best to hide their affairs because of their fears of losing their shirts in a divorce. Locker room talk as grown men differed from the boyhood chatter about who was hot and who was not because grown men were more interested in protecting their assets. Obviously her ex's lawyer had found a way to keep her from getting the lion's share. At least that's what he assumed, based on the little Allie had told him.

He couldn't help feeling sorry for Madison. And her kids. The kids most of all. Sure, they were brats, but the snide comments attacking their mother with their father's words told him that they'd been the biggest losers in the divorce. Still, it didn't make their actions right.

Them coming here was a good thing. Enid wouldn't put up with their garbage. Hopefully, a life outside their privileged world would show the kids that there was more to being happy than having all the latest gadgets.

He'd returned to Arcadia Valley to escape all that. He'd grown up here, feeling like a misfit because he was so much smarter than all the other kids. He'd started his own software company and made his first million by the time he was nineteen. But by twenty-nine, he was disillusioned and burned out, with millions to show for it, but not a single person he could truly count on, except for his friend Liam. Everyone wanted something from him, and it always involved his checkbook.

He sold the company and returned here, buying the old farm where he'd grown up, even though his mother now lived in the memory care unit at Retro Village. Most days, she didn't remember who he was, and he didn't blame her. In the early years of his success, instead of spending time with her, he'd sent her checks. Yes, her forgetfulness now was Alzheimer's talking. But maybe if he'd been a better son, she would remember him more clearly in her lucid moments.

Though everyone here knew he'd built a successful business, most of them assumed he'd come back because he'd somehow lost it all. And he liked that. When he was a kid, they all treated him like a freak because he did calculus problems for fun. When everyone knew he was rich, he didn't know if any of his friends were real. And now that he lived in a tiny house he built himself and spent most of his days helping the Bigbys on the farm, he knew what friendship was. The people who saw beyond the beard and old clothes and took the time to talk to him anyway, those were the people he cared most about.

So why couldn't he get Madison McKay out of his mind? She wasn't likely to be interested in a man like him, not when she clearly came from everything he'd run from. He'd seen the distasteful way she looked at him when they first met, taking her time to warm up to him.

Maybe it was the warm way she had embraced Enid or the way her face had lit up as she and Allie met in person for the first time. She wasn't what you would call model pretty, and if he was right in his suspicion about her being a Silicon Valley divorcee, he could see why someone younger would be more appealing. He shook his head. Actually, he thought Madison was a lot prettier than the women who had chased him during his successes. She didn't wear a lot of makeup or look like she'd had much work done. And while some might call her a little chubby, he liked that she wasn't so stick thin that he was afraid he'd break her.

What was he doing?

Madison wasn't his to evaluate. Sure, she was available. Allie had told him she was divorced. He wasn't the kind of guy to reject a woman for being divorced. But he also wasn't looking for a project. The weariness in her eyes told him that she was still recovering from whatever had happened. Clearly, the kids were still in fight mode. And Wade was done with being in relationships where there wasn't an equal give-and-take.

The women he'd dated, if they weren't after his money, had all seemed to see him as an answer to their problems. He didn't mind helping people, but was it too much to ask for to have a woman who wanted to spend time with him simply because she liked his company?

He shook his head, then walked to the large freezer the Bigbys let him keep in their barn. Living in a tiny house, while it felt good to be self-reliant and have only the most basic belongings, he was short on space for a freezer to keep all his meat. His dad had taught him to hunt as a boy, and part of his self-reliance lifestyle was that he only ate food he grew or hunted himself. And all right, Enid often supplemented his diet with things she'd prepared, but he knew the Bigbys were also committed to eating as much local and fresh as they could.

A noise made him turn. Madison. He should have known that thinking about her would somehow send a signal into the universe that he wanted to see her. There was a reason the Bible cautioned people about thinking only of the good things of God. People often didn't realize how powerful their thoughts were, but he did. And, once again he'd proven himself right.

"Hi," she said. "I saw you come in here, and I wanted to say..."

She paused, staring down at the meat packet in his hand. "Venison? Is that deer?"

"Right off this property. I get tags from fish and game, so it's all legal. I don't know if you've met your cousin Caroline yet, but she and her husband, Hayden, are putting together special packages for the hunters in the fall. Wildlife is abundant in this area, so they're trying to capitalize on all the benefits of being connected to nature."

Her face turned white, and he realized he'd probably said too much. Sometimes he forgot that city people were less inclined to understand that part of the balance of living in nature also involved carefully controlling the wildlife population.

"Do you know how many times we've seen the cartoon about the baby deer that loses his mother? I don't think I could eat, you know," she said.

He shrugged. "This isn't a cartoon character, and this buck was much older than he would have been."

"And you think eating his dad is any better?" The incredulous look on her face made him glad he hadn't added that if she wanted to see the trophy to prove it, she'd find it for sale in the gift shop. Wade wasn't one to save them, but some people thought that having a deer head hanging in their home was a status symbol. He didn't need the status, so if it made a guy feel better to say he'd gone hunting and brought this back, well, more power to him. And, it gave Wade a little more extra money to go toward some of the projects he liked to support. Anonymously, of course.

Since selling his company, Wade had given away millions of dollars to various charities. He believed God had blessed him with so much money for a reason, and that reason was to share it with others. That's how he viewed everything that came into his hands. It wasn't his to cling to, but something for him to take care of for a while until he could see where God meant for it to be. Kind of like his old farmhouse. He had no reason to live there, not when the little house he built himself was more than adequate. But it had given Allie and her husband Cole a place to call their own, making room in Enid's house for Madison and her family.

Wade looked down at the bundle in his hands. "I'm pretty sure this fellow didn't father a cartoon character. And, if we don't manage the wildlife in our area, they will grow too numerous, and it will harm the ecosystem. I know it's hard for someone to understand killing what looks like a sweet animal, but in my opinion, it's no different from the beef, pork, or chicken you have on your dinner plate every night."

For a moment, Madison looked thoughtful. "I suppose, but none of them have faces or stories that make me relate to them."

"Fair enough. That's why I keep emphasizing that the one you love was a cartoon character. Just one deer. Also why I like pointing out that if we don't have careful management of our wildlife, we might lose more animals to starvation and disease because the land can't support the growing population."

"I hadn't thought of it that way," she said. "Thank you for taking the time to explain to me."

Keeping his distance from her was going to be a lot harder, now that he was seeing her as a human being rather than a caricature. Almost the reverse of what they were talking about here. People objected to eating deer because of stories like the popular children's movie, but they didn't understand the greater picture.

Getting to know Madison, she wasn't just the statistic of yet another Silicon Valley wife thrown away, but a real human being who'd been hurt by some thoughtless jerk.

Madison smiled at him. "I just wanted to apologize for what my son said earlier, and to thank you for your encouraging words. It's been really hard on them, their father leaving. I don't usually share personal details with strangers, but

Allie says you're a good family friend. My husband left just after Christmas, never returning from a business trip. He sent me an email, telling me he needed to find himself. A lawyer showed up the next day with divorce papers. Other than a few emails he's sent me regarding the divorce, we haven't heard from him since."

Ouch. None of the guys he'd known had ever been so cold.

"I'm sorry to hear that. What about custody, support, and all that?"

Madison let out a long sigh. "Having children makes him feel too tied down. Technically, I'm entitled to support, but good luck finding him. He's gone off to live at some ashram in India with his yoga instructor. Because he claims he's given up all material possessions, he no longer has a phone or computer with which to communicate."

The discouragement in her voice was evident. "So ironic, considering he'd charged thousands of dollars to our credit cards for Christmas. How does someone go from being so materialistic one month to claiming possessions are the root of all unhappiness only a few weeks later?"

On one hand, Wade would have to agree about the idea of possessions being the root of a lot of unhappiness in people's lives. But Madison was right that her ex had clearly gone about it in a convoluted way.

Then she shook her head. "I'm sorry. That was probably too much information. I just wanted you to know that the kids aren't bad, they're just really hurt, and without their father giving them answers, they're lashing out at everyone. It's not personal."

She looked so broken. Like she'd lost everything. And maybe, she had. Reading between the lines of what Madison and Allie had told him, she probably had nothing left to her name. Just her kids. And the older two were probably making it very difficult for her to find any comfort in having them.

"I know. And I don't mean to overstep, but just because they're hurting, it doesn't give them the excuse to hurt you."

For a moment, she looked like she was going to argue with him, but then she nodded. "In theory, yes. But what am I supposed to do? It's bad enough that their father left. I can't bring myself to tell them the horrible things he said."

He didn't have any answers for her. What did he know? He didn't have any kids, though he did spend time working with the youth group at church.

"I wish I had wisdom for you. I think you're probably right not to tell the children everything. But you also can't let them talk to others the way they did earlier today."

Tears filled her eyes. "I just don't know how. In the past, I would do things like take away their electronics or other privileges. But it's not just me who's lost everything. They have, too. There's nothing left to punish them with."

When he was a kid, he hadn't had electronics or any of the other little gadgets kids these days had. He learned computers and technology by scavenging other people's scraps and building his own out of them. It's how he'd developed his software company. He couldn't afford to buy it, and he was too ethical to steal it, so he created his own. He'd always thought that kids these days lacked that kind of imagination and ingenuity. None of them seemed to understand the value of hard work. Maybe the situation with Madison's kids wasn't exactly the same as the other Silicon Valley brats he'd known, but there sure were a lot of similarities.

"Could I make a suggestion?" he asked.

Madison brushed away the tears in her eyes and squared her shoulders, like she was trying to escape whatever emotion it stirred up in her. He'd like to tell her she didn't have to hide, but honestly, he was already involving himself too deeply in the life of a woman who still needed very much to find herself. Funny that he used the same words her ex did, except that they were true. She'd probably had a firm grip on herself and her life, but that had been turned upside down, and she needed to figure out what the new life she was building for herself looked like. Without building it around someone else.

"As long as you're not offended if I don't take it." The small smile she gave him made him like her even more. Her ex had crushed a lot of things in her, but he could still see the strength of her spirit peeking out.

"Maybe if your kids learned how to serve others, they wouldn't be so focused on having everyone else serve them. Once a month, I take the youth group to volunteer at Corrina's Cupboard, where they serve the homeless in our community. Your daughter has a lot of disdain for homeless people, maybe it's time she met them."

Madison nodded slowly. "Our old church sometimes went to the local soup kitchen to help out, but Dave would never let me bring the kids. He was afraid they would get some kind of disease."

The sadness in her voice made him wish he could do more for her. More for her kids. They'd been taught to fear homeless people, and as he glanced down at his own appearance, he could see why they'd been so rude to him. Today wasn't the first time he'd been mistaken for someone who was homeless, and mostly, he didn't mind. The thing that bothered him was that if he shaved, cut his hair, and threw on a suit, people like these kids would treat him a lot differently. Was it so wrong to want people to spend more time looking at the inside than the outside?

"Are you afraid they'll get a disease?" he asked.

She gave a small laugh, and it warmed him. Just that slight

hint was enough to make him want to figure out how to get her laughing more.

"No more than I am in sending them to school. That place is a veritable germ factory. I'm amazed at all the bugs they bring home. But that's life. I could keep them in an insulated bubble all the time so they would never get sick. But then they would miss out on so much. A few viruses here and there is worth the price of living, don't you think?"

He liked this woman. A lot. Maybe, if she stuck around for a while, and found healing to move on with her life...

What was he doing? There were a lot of maybes and what ifs in that wish. That was just as bad as putting yourself in a bubble and insulating yourself from life.

"I agree. So maybe next time I take the youth group on a service project, your kids could come?"

"I'd like that a lot. People in our old church were not very understanding about the divorce. But Allie says that Arcadia Valley community church treats people like family and they're not going to judge us for Dave's actions. I think what my kids need the most is to know that even though their dad didn't do right by them, they still have a Father in Heaven who loves them very much. It's the only hope that keeps me going. I have to believe that even though nothing in my life makes sense, there is still a God who loves us and wants the very best for us. If what I thought was the best was taken from us, surely that means God has a better plan somewhere. I just have to hang on long enough to see it come to pass."

Who was he kidding? Every word out of Madison's mouth made him like her just a little bit more. But hearing her depth of faith was like God continually hitting him over the head, reminding him that this was exactly the kind of woman he'd been asking for. He'd wanted a woman who loved God more than all the other garbage every other woman seemed to put stock in. And here was Madison, having lost everything, but with the faith that in the midst of everything going wrong, God was still there.

"I believe it will," he said, fighting the lump forming in his throat. "Jesus said that faith the size of a mustard seed could move mountains, so surely faith as strong as yours will give you the strength for whatever you need in the future."

"I agree," Enid's voice rang out. "I prayed for twenty-seven years, three months, two weeks, and a day that I would see my Adam's daughter again. And here you are. I knew that God could say no, and I would have accepted that answer. But I am the most blessed woman alive to see this dream come true. Those children of yours are squabbling again, and I've always believed that idle hands make for idle minds, which is the source of all disharmony in the world."

Then Enid grinned. "That, and gluten. I can tell by the way your children act that you have fed them entirely too much junk food in their lives. They're not going to like it, but we're going to do a family cleanse."

Wade fought the urge to groan. He'd been around the Bigbys long enough to know that Enid's cleanses were the stuff of legends. Mostly because, as Allie often pointed out, none of them had any backing in scientific evidence. And yet, Enid persisted in making everyone in her home follow whatever bizarre diet she'd decided on.

"Not all cleanses are good for a child's growing dietary needs," Madison said. "I'm happy to consider it if you lay out exactly what the cleanse consists of and how you believe it will benefit the children. I realize I'm in no position to make demands, however, I want to be sure all of their nutritional needs are met with a balanced meal plan."

Wow. From the look on Enid's face, she was thinking the same thing. Madison was a little tiger. She'd clearly gotten a lot of her genes from Enid. At the very least, her strength of will.

"Rutabagas are good for the soul," Enid said.

"I quite agree," Madison said. "However, they don't contain all of the nutrients necessary for a growing body and mind. So let's talk about other healthy foods we can incorporate into this cleanse of yours."

Enid's mouth opened like she was going to retort, but then closed again as she appeared to be struggling to come up with one. Allie entered the room and put her arm around her grandmother.

"It's exactly what I've been telling you for years," Allie said. "Now that I have an ally, maybe you'll start listening to reason. Otherwise, I'm going to call Layla and have her bring in that nutritionist friend of hers to go over exactly what you've been eating."

Enid nodded slowly as Allie turned to Madison. "You weren't here for the big drama, but Gram is dealing with some health issues and we're working very hard at maintaining a balanced diet for optimal health. I don't know if you remember me telling you about Layla, my brother Andrew's wife, but I'm sure you'll meet her soon. They're off visiting her father, otherwise, they'd have been here to greet you."

Okay, so Madison wasn't the only one to inherit Enid's strength of character. That's what he liked about all the Bigbys. At least Enid and her grandchildren. Enid's children, well, they were slowly growing on Wade. When Wade had first returned to Arcadia Valley, the Bigby children were fighting to put Enid in a home and wrestle control of the farm from her and the grandchildren. They'd believed Enid mentally incompetent and, he suspected, were hoping to steal her estate to milk it for all that it was worth. However, Enid's granddaughter, Caroline, worked out a plan with her now husband, Hayden, to turn Bigby Farm into a guest experience where people came to stay on the farm in tiny houses and learn about farm life. While the operation was still in its infancy, it was already turning a profit. Allie used the farm for her growing lavender business, an endeavor that had only been a hobby until recent months, but was now starting to be a profitable business. Andrew, Enid's grandson and Allie's brother, helped his sister and cousin with their various business operations in between the classes he was taking in nearby Twin Falls to become a grief counselor.

Though Wade had initially come to Bigby Farm to help with odds and ends, the family was pushing him to take on a bigger role as farm manager. In addition to the overnight guests, Bigby Farm hosted summer day camps as well as other opportunities for children and families to experience traditional farming. Which was great, except that also meant they had the various herbs and vegetables the farm produced that needed to be sold. As the farm expanded, each person following their passion, it seemed like everyone's work load was becoming more than what they could handle.

Which gave him an idea.

He turned to Madison, who was listening as Allie finished her story about how Layla and Andrew had gotten together.

"I don't mean to interrupt, but I just thought of a way to handle the children." He smiled at Enid, who he was counting on to be an ally in his plan. "What if we assigned the children various chores on the farm? Though Allie has people helping her with the lavender operation, and Caroline has the same for our guest program and day camp, I'm struggling to keep up with the day to day farm tasks. Since Allie needed help getting some of her lavender repotted today, I didn't have enough time to work in the herb beds the way I usually do."

As he looked at the women, he could see the concern furrowing their brows. He knew what Enid and Allie were thinking, and their objections would be easy to overcome. Hopefully, he could convince Madison.

"I'm not complaining, mind you. June is always a busy time on the farm. I don't mind the work. But a few extra hands will make it lighter, and perhaps it will teach the children a lesson in appreciating everything that goes into what they have."

Madison looked thoughtful, but the expression on Allie's face hadn't changed.

"I told you to hire someone to help with the farm," she said. "You shouldn't be taking all of this on yourself."

"I'm not. I've put out an ad to get some extra help. Like I said, it's a busy time of year. I know the extra work is temporary. I wasn't saying this to complain, but to point out that there are opportunities for the children. They can learn how to repot plants, attach labels for your products, weed Enid's garden, feed the animals, and help with other easy tasks on the farm."

Allie nodded slowly. "As long as I'm not taking advantage. I don't want you ever to think that we don't appreciate you."

"I would never think that," he assured her. "I love what I do here, and I'd keep doing it even if you stopped paying me."

Enid grinned at him. She'd been part of the many fights he'd had with the Bigby cousins over his salary. He didn't want their money, didn't need it. He'd started helping them even before they could pay him, because he liked the work and he liked the family. The more money they gave them, the more he gave away. He didn't want to take any more of their profits than he had to since they needed it more than he did. Extra profits meant they could expand their businesses as well as maintain the farm these businesses were designed to protect. That had been the driving force behind all these great ideas the cousins were now putting into action. Saving Bigby Farm.

"All right," Allie said. "But let's see what we can do to hire someone else to help you. Maybe another general handy person."

"I'll do it," Madison said. "I know you invited me here to stay as long as I needed to get back on my feet. But I've never felt right taking charity. Everyone accuses me of being lazy and not finding work. I don't know anything about farming, but I'm willing to learn. The kids can help me and maybe they'll see how wrong they were in their insults toward me. Plus, it sounds like most of those tasks I can do and keep Hope with me. That way I don't have to find daycare."

From the way Enid and Allie looked at Madison, Wade could tell they held her in the same high regard he did. She was an amazing woman, willing to do whatever it took for her family. She wasn't looking for someone to rescue her, but for a way to help herself. And her kids.

"That sounds just like the way I grew up," Enid said. "Everyone pitching in, even the little ones. But when it's not convenient to have Hope with you, I'm happy to take her. In fact, I insist. It's been far too long since I've had a little one to spoil, and I want to make up for lost time with your children."

Allie nodded. "We'll all help with the children. I know you're the kind of person to take responsibility for yourself, but you're with family now. I'm happy to let you take the position I just asked Wade to find someone to fill. Part of our vision is to give jobs to people who need them but can't always work in a traditional way. My assistant is a single mother I used to work with who got fired because of her childcare issues. So she brings her kids to work and they help out here. And when the children can't be involved, one of us finds a way to keep them entertained."

Once again, he could see Madison fighting tears. Maybe someday she would realize that she didn't have to always be so strong.

"Thank you," Madison said. "You don't know what this means to me. Figuring out what to do with the children was my biggest worry about going to work. I didn't want to stay here and sponge off you forever."

Allie hugged her, and while Wade felt a twinge of envy, he was also glad to see the connection between the two women. When he'd first met Madison, she seemed lost. But now, she seemed like she was finally seeing her way.

Then Allie turned to him. "Since you're the farm manager and you know where we need help, I'm putting Madison under your supervision. Put together a list of tasks and show her what needs to be done."

Smiling at Madison, Allie continued. "I don't expect you to become perfect overnight. Just do your best and ask for help where you need it. There's no one I trust more with this farm than Wade."

High praise, but as Wade felt Enid's eyes upon him, he wondered if that trust had been misplaced. He knew what Enid was thinking. The old woman had been relentless in matching up her grandchildren and was now equally strong in her demands to have great-grandchildren. A man would have to be a fool to think that she wasn't looking at Wade and Madison and wondering how to get them together. Given his previous thoughts about Madison and his growing respect for her, he didn't entirely mind. Except the more he looked at her and thought about all the things he liked about her, the more it frightened him. She was someone he could actually come to care for in a romantic way.

But was her heart ready for someone new? Would her kids be willing to let go of their anger at the divorce enough to let them find happiness? And if this wasn't the right time, could his heart handle the pain of risking and losing? He was tired of women seeing him as a stepping stone to the next thing. He wasn't going to pursue someone who didn't see him as her future.

It was too soon to be thinking these thoughts. It was safe enough for Enid to consider, because her heart didn't stand to be broken. For Wade, however, he'd do his best to keep a professional distance and work to get Madison trained to be self-sufficient on her jobs so he wouldn't need to supervise.

CHAPTER 3

a month after starting work at Bigby Farm, Madison finally felt like her muscles were starting to get used to the hard work. Actually, she woke up craving the experience. The forty-pound bag of chicken feed that she used to struggle to get over to the chicken coop was easier to lift, and today, as she carried it from the barn to the chicken coop without having to stop and catch her breath, she felt a sense of accomplishment she hadn't felt in a long time.

She turned to tell Wade, but then she remembered that he'd left her alone to feed the animals today while he ran some errands. But it didn't matter. The kids were waiting for her at the gate, and while they hadn't embraced the change of life the way she had, at least they could appreciate that she'd done this task all by herself.

"Can you guys believe I did it? I didn't even need the wagon to bring this up here." She smiled at the kids, but they scowled back.

"You're still fat," D.J. said.

Her son had never called her fat before. But she supposed he'd heard his father do it all the time.

"That wasn't very nice," she said, giving him a stern look. "Nor was it the point of what I was saying. I just thought you would all be proud of me for how strong I'm getting."

D.J.'s expression didn't waver. "I don't care about that. I just want you to get skinny again so Dad will take us back."

The second reference to her weight stung, but not as much now that she knew why her son was so obsessed with it. This wasn't about her, but about the fact that he missed his father.

"And why do you think it will matter?" Maybe if he could see how ridiculous his theory was, he would understand that his father wasn't coming back.

"Because I heard him on the phone before he left. He told whoever it was that you were a disgusting fat cow and he was tired of pretending," D.J. said.

She hadn't known about that conversation, or that her son had overheard it. What a horrible thing for a child to think. Actually, it was a horrible thing for a husband to think about his wife.

"I'm sure you misunderstood," she said softly.

"No I didn't. He said the only reason he was waiting for the divorce was so it wouldn't ruin Christmas."

At least now she understood why D.J. had been so subdued that day. Why, despite being lavished with all the expensive gifts and everything on his Christmas list, he'd been so angry. And when she'd served dessert, he'd refused it, saying that sweets make people fat.

Madison turned and looked at Faith. "Did you know about this?"

Eyes full of tears, Faith nodded.

Her poor kids. They'd been keeping this from her for so long. No wonder they were so angry.

"Did you talk to your dad about it?" Madison asked.

They shook their heads.

"Did he say anything directly to you guys about us getting divorced or him leaving?"

Once again, they shook their heads.

Basically, the kids overheard a conversation and extrapolated it in their own way, making her the bad guy since he'd never explained anything to them or to her. No wonder the kids were confused. What was she supposed to tell them?

The truth was too much.

She gestured to a nearby bench. "Let's talk."

They followed her and sat.

"I know I've gained weight. But let me ask you something. Am I different person because I weigh more?"

The kids looked at each other, then back at her. "You spend more time with Hope than you do with us," D.J. said.

"But is that because I'm fat, or because she's a baby?"

She deliberately used that word—fat— hoping the kids would understand that her weight was not the issue.

"I've been trying to lose weight so Daddy will come back," Faith whispered.

Madison squeezed her eyes shut. How many times had she dismissed her daughter's insistence that she wasn't hungry as her becoming a picky eater? Or on the stress of her father's leaving?

"You do not need to lose weight," Madison said. "The doctor said you were healthy at your last appointment. If you needed to lose weight, the doctor would have said so. The only person who gets to say that we need to lose weight is the doctor, and it's a medical issue."

It was a good thing Dave wasn't here, because she would slap him silly. It was one thing to have her children thinking that he'd left her because of her weight. But to have a child thinking there was something wrong with her and that her weight made him not want to be with them, that was inexcusable. What kind of father did that to a child?

She'd thought she'd known him, but clearly, she hadn't had a clue. Wherever he was, she hoped that he would someday understand the damage he'd done to the children. And somehow, make it up to them.

Yes, it hurt, being made fun of for her weight. But mostly, she felt sad for the man who would tell others such things. Was that all people were to him? He was the one who would wake up one morning and realize how empty his life was because of the value he placed in temporary things. He'd always been a good-looking man, but one day his looks would fade, then where would he be? But how was she supposed to teach that to her children? Help them see that things their father valued were worthless?

They'd been going to church with Gram. Would it be wrong of her to talk to the pastor about talking to the children about body image?

Not just the children, but all of them. Surely she wasn't the only one who struggled with her weight. However, she was at least secure enough in herself to know that her weight was not who she was, that it was just a number, and that her extra curves had no reflection on who she was as a person.

They finished feeding the chickens, and the children remained silent. From the smirks D.J. kept tossing Faith, she was pretty sure he thought he'd scored a few points. Somehow she had to get her son to understand that it wasn't about scoring points. And that his words could genuinely hurt someone else. More importantly, he had to know that what he did was wrong.

As they walked back to the house, she put her arm around Faith. "I want you to promise me to eat more. I know you think you're fat, but I think you're a beautiful little girl, and you're perfect, just as you are."

Faith wrenched away from her grasp. "Stop saying that. You're just trying to make it better for you. You made him leave. And even if you're not willing to do what it takes to get him back, I'm going to."

She ran off toward the house, D.J. following behind. She tried not to let their words hurt, but they did. She'd done everything to make her marriage work, including counseling. Dave hadn't wanted to go. He'd skipped more meetings than he'd made, and he'd made it clear from day one that he was not invested in trying to save their marriage. What was she supposed to have done about that? She'd read all the books, tried all the tactics, but nothing could make a man want to stay if he didn't want to.

Their marriage had been limping along even prior to his leaving, so it wasn't entirely a surprise. The way he'd done it had just stunk.

The children went into the house, where they would likely try to find something to do, declare everything suggested to be boring, then start tormenting each other.

As selfish as it sounded, she didn't have the energy to deal with it right now. Slowing her steps, she prayed, asking God to give her some wisdom on what to do next. She'd already thought of talking to the pastor, and taking Faith into the doctor, so a medical professional could tell her that she wasn't fat, but what could she do in these immediate moments?

She hadn't gotten very far when Wade approached. "How's it going? I could use your help with getting the shipments ready, if you finished everything else."

Right. She was supposed to be working, not dealing with her family tragedies.

"Yes. I can help. Just tell me what you need."

Wade took her gently by the arm. "Is everything all right? You look like you've just received some terrible news."

In a way, she had. How was she supposed to confess to another person about her weight? Or how awful her children had just been? Fortunately, Wade had been very under-standing in the past.

"In a manner of speaking, yes. D.J. lashed out at me, and he confessed some things that I hadn't known that he felt led to the divorce. Faith confirmed it, and I'm not sure what to do. The children have some weird ideas about why our marriage ended, and I don't know how to clarify things. I've tried to keep them out of my relationship with my ex-husband, but they're firmly in it, and it doesn't seem fair to tell them things that might make them hate their father."

Wade ran his fingers through his hair. "Wow. That's a tough one. Divorce is hard on kids, and I can see where they might get some funny ideas. What did they say?"

The sympathy on his face made her feel a little less hesi-tant about confessing her insecurity. "Apparently D.J. over-heard his father telling someone on the phone that the reason he was leaving me was because I was fat. Faith has been starving herself because she thinks she's too fat, and if she and I both get skinny again their father will take me back."

She could hardly keep her voice from shaking as tears stung the backs of her eyes. Wade pulled her into a hug. She hadn't expected the gesture, but it was strangely comforting.

"That's crazy talk, and you know it. People don't get divorced because of weight issues. But it sounds like your kids are really hurting, and they took it out on you."

It had been a long time since anyone had hugged her like that, just letting her know that she wasn't alone. Because most the time, she felt like she was.

"Thank you. That means a lot."

She pulled away and wiped the tears from her eyes. "Logi-cally, I know what you said is true, but it doesn't keep it from hurting. I mean, let's face it. I am overweight. But I'd like to think that even though my pant size might have changed a lot, who I am inside hasn't."

Wade looked her up and down. "You look just fine to me. Sure, you've got some curves, but what healthy woman doesn't? I like that you're not one of those vain, pampered women who spend so much time on their bodies that they neglect their minds. I like you just the way you are. And if you pardon me for being so blunt, any man who would think otherwise is an idiot."

He was just saying it to be nice, because she knew she wasn't the most attractive woman on the planet. Still, it was nice of Wade to say so.

"Thanks. But that doesn't solve what I have to do about my kids. How do I teach them better body image? And how do I say that their father was being a jerk, without putting him down? He's their father, and I don't want to be rude or disrespectful of him or mess with their relationship in any way."

He smiled at her and patted her arm. "You just keep on doing what you're doing. A lot of people don't have that kind of sense in a divorce, and they do their best to make kids feel torn. But you just keep loving the kids, and letting them know that it's okay to love both you and their father, and it'll be all right."

The breeze picked up, and she shivered slightly. Wade took off his flannel shirt and handed it to her. "Take this. It's not quite T-shirt weather, and I've got my thermal underneath. A little hot for both, but it wasn't this morning when I got up."

She put his shirt on, and it felt good to be wrapped in such coziness. Heat from his body, the fabric, and just the warmth of a person caring about her. And, it was nice that the shirt actually fit. Had it been one of Dave's, it would've been too tight, proof that she was a little bigger than she ought to be.

"Thank you. I'd been working in the house prior to this, so I hadn't noticed that it was a little chilly out. I was doing a lot of cleaning, helping Gram out."

Then she gave a small smile. "My cardio for the day."

But instead of laughing with her, he shook his head. "Everything we do is cardio. If you want your kids to have healthy body image, then you need to stop thinking badly about yourself and your size. You're a beautiful woman, and I can't imagine that you would be any more beautiful if you were thinner. Love yourself in the body that you have, and they'll learn the same."

She looked down at the ground. She'd been trying to keep the conversation off her body. "You're just saying that to make me feel better."

"No, I'm not. I know I shouldn't say this, but I find you very attractive. If it wouldn't be crossing a big line, I'd even ask you out."

The air around her stilled. Had he just really said that?

She looked up at him. "You would want to go out with me?"

He shoved his hands in his pockets as he nodded. "Yeah. But I know the timing isn't right, with you being newly divorced and all, and me technically being your boss, and the closeness of our families, it just seems like a bad idea."

Then he looked deep into her eyes. "But I'd be lying if I said I didn't spend an inappropriate amount of time thinking about kissing those lips of yours. And your husband was a fool for thinking differently."

He turned and walked away, muttering about being an idiot, and she wasn't entirely sure which idiot he was talking about.

Dave? Her? Or maybe even him, for confessing those feelings when he just said what a bad idea it was. But as much as she'd have liked to have found out, she let him go, because he was right. All those reasons for him not asking her out more were exactly the reasons why she shouldn't pursue him either.

CHAPTER 4

*W*hat had he been thinking, telling Madison all that? It was like he'd gone and unsharpened all the tools in the shed. But what else was he supposed to say when a perfectly attractive woman was down on herself for thinking she was fat? Worse, when her stinking ex was telling people he'd left her for it?

Silicon Valley had been rough, but not that rough. Or maybe he'd just been out of the rat race for too long.

As he rounded the corner of the house, he saw the kids huddled together, a tiny plume of smoke between them.

What were they doing?

He ran to them and could see they were playing with matches. Surely they knew better.

"Hey!"

D.J. spun and glared at him. "What?"

"What are you doing with those matches?"

"None of your business." D.J. kicked some dirt on the tiny fire he'd built.

Faith looked scared. "You said we weren't going to get caught."

"Shut up."

D.J. shot her a menacing glare, then turned back to him. "Get back to work. No wonder you're homeless, putting your nose in other people's business instead of doing your job."

Was this a kid talking? He sounded like a puppet of all those snotty execs he'd left behind. If D.J. had been a man, Wade would have given him the what-for. But this was a kid, clinging to what little he had left of a father who'd disappeared.

"This is my job," Wade said quietly. "Taking care of the farm and protecting it. That little fire you're building could ruin everything."

He pointed to the new barn.

"And?" D.J.'s haughty tone made him want to shake the kid. But he was just a kid, and he didn't know any better.

"Our main barn burned down over Christmas, and the family could have lost everything. Which is why we're careful about fire here. One careless move, and everything your family has ever worked for could be destroyed."

D.J. scowled at him. "They're not my family. And I don't care about your stupid barn. And Christmas is stupid anyway."

Wade closed his eyes for a moment, and sent a quick prayer heavenward. He'd forgotten that Christmas had been when their family had fallen apart.

But that didn't excuse the boy's rudeness. At some point, these kids had to learn that their pain didn't give them an excuse to hurt others.

"They are your family, and I'm sorry you can't see that. But you should be grateful for them, because they love you very much."

He knew his words weren't going to change D.J.s mind, but it was disheartening to see the boy's anger.

D.J.'s glare deepened. "She should've brought us to my dad, not this rathole."

Bigby Farm was hardly a rathole. True, a few years ago, some people might have said that. But Caroline, Andrew, Allie, and their families had worked very hard to change things. They'd done an excellent job and were a testament to the true power of human determination and faith in their dreams.

Unfortunately, those weren't values the boy's father had taught him.

"So where is he, then? You've set your father up on this great pedestal, but let me ask you, when your mom was struggling to make things work, where was he? When it came to saving you from this rathole, where was he? Why haven't you heard from him at all since he left?"

D.J. didn't answer, and Wade hadn't expected him to. But the boy had to realize that the true test of love was actually being there for the person he claimed to love.

"If I had a son, or anyone I loved, I wouldn't go so long without talking to them. And I wouldn't let them go away to some rathole, as you call it."

D.J. charged at him. "My dad loves me. You don't know anything."

He had probably been too strong in his criticism of D.J.'s father, and he should have chosen his words better. But someone had to make him see that D.J. was wrong in punishing his mother for his father's actions. And even though he was but a small boy, the fists pummeling Wade were strong.

Wade took a step back. "I'm sorry. I'm sure your father does love you in his way. I just think that if he loved you the way you say he does, he would be here for you."

He rubbed his side with the boy had hit him. "And I think you know that, too. If you believed in your father's love, you would have been strong enough in that feeling that you wouldn't have needed to hit me. It's not okay to hit."

"So what? Are you going to tell on me to my mom? Like I care. If it wasn't for her and her fat butt, we'd still be in our old house, and our dad would still be there."

Part of him had hoped that she'd been exaggerating or misunderstood what her son had said when she'd expressed her pain over his actions. But here he was, hearing it for himself. The wounded child who thought that a marriage was made or broken over someone's weight.

"It takes two people to make a marriage work," he said. "Maybe that's the excuse your dad gave, but what was he doing to be loving and kind to her?"

D.J. shook his head. "Who could love a fat pig?"

Wade glanced over at Faith, who had tears running down her cheeks. This perfect, sweet little girl who thought something was wrong with her because she wasn't thin enough.

"I could. Your mother is a beautiful woman, but more than that, she is a kind woman. She has a good heart, and that's what I would look for in a partner."

The arrogant look on D.J.'s face only deepened. "Of course she would say that. Look at you. Homeless. No woman would ever want you."

As he glanced over at his reflection in the window, he had to admit that the boy had a point. At least in the fact that his exterior was a little scary. Maybe he had gone a little too far in rejecting his outward appearance.

"Beauty starts on the inside," he said, turning his gaze back to Faith. "Don't believe the lies about what's on the outside as being important. You never know what's on the inside."

Faith shook her head. "D.J. is right. You don't know anything."

It was clear he wasn't going to get through to either child.

Not now. Not with the way he looked. A few years ago, in the boardroom in his custom suits, he could convince anyone of his importance. But now, he was just some farmhand, a few steps above being homeless. But maybe that was what the kids needed to see. Maybe it was time for them to understand that appearances weren't always what they seemed.

He looked over the remains of the fire, making sure it was all out. Fortunately, the kids hadn't done much, but he still went over to the spigot, grabbed the hose, and thoroughly watered it down.

"Since you guys don't seem to respect things around here, I'm going to teach you some," Wade said.

The cocky expression returned to Dylan's face. "What? Are you going to beat us? I'll call a lawyer faster than you can get over here."

This kid had definitely been raised by a Silicon Valley snob. Wade shook his head.

"No. I don't believe in hitting people. Unlike you."

He rubbed his side, where the boy had hit him. It didn't hurt, but that didn't matter. D.J.'s actions were still wrong.

"I think you need to spend some time working, to learn where all of the things you have come from," Wade said.

"We don't have anything," Faith said quietly.

He'd watched these children sit and watch their mother as she struggled to do chores around the farm. While Madison had grown stronger, the two of them just sat and watched her, critiquing her constantly. Even baby Hope helped more than they did. That was going to change now. He just hoped that Madison wouldn't get too mad at him for it.

"The two of you are going to start pulling your own weight around here. When you grow up on a farm, everyone helps out, even the youngest members of the family. Hope helps your mom, but you two do not. That changes today."

The kids stared at him blankly.

"Every day, I'm going to give you a list of chores. You will do them, and you will do them properly, or you will do them again."

"Make us," D.J. said.

Wade shrugged. "I understand that your Aunt Allie lets you play with her iPad sometimes. I'll be speaking to her about not letting you use it until your chores are done."

"She's not our aunt," D.J. said. "And who cares about a stupid iPad?"

The family had thought calling Madison's cousins aunts and uncles would be easier on the children, but they obviously hadn't counted on the children's stubbornness.

"Fine. But let me assure you that every fun thing you've been allowed while here will be taken away. Now, today's chore is that I need you to clean the chicken coop. Take out all the bedding and put it in the compost pile. And when you're done, come get me, so I can make sure that you have done it correctly. When that's done, you put in new bedding. Now, let me show you where the tools are."

It was a task he'd been intending to give Madison this afternoon, but he'd noticed that she'd done a very nice job of organizing the displays in the gift shop. If she could bring Allie's stockroom to a similar sort of order, it would make everyone's lives easier. He'd just felt guilty asking her, when there were other pressing matters to be dealt with.

"We're not cleaning the chicken coop. Mom smells disgusting when she does it."

So they had noticed. Well, now they were going to notice a little more. On themselves.

"Good. So you know what to do then."

He started toward the barn and indicated the children should follow him. But they remained standing where they were.

"Okay then, fine. But I'm going into town later, and I was

going to take your mom and the rest of you for ice cream. However, if it's not done by the time I'm ready to leave, you won't get any."

He actually hadn't been planning on taking them out for ice cream, but he knew how Enid refused to keep sweets in the house, and the children often complained about wanting them. If they weren't motivated by losing privileges, maybe gaining something would. However, the children looked bored.

"Suit yourself. But there it is. You don't want to do the work, you don't get the ice cream. And you don't get any fun either."

Then, remembering how the children had just been occupying themselves with fun, he held out his hand. "Now, give me the matches or lighter or whatever it was that you were using to start the fire."

D.J. stared at him, but Faith looked worried. "I heard about the old barn burning down. I didn't think of that when D.J. said it would be fun to light these anthills on fire."

So that's what they were doing. Faith looked like she had a little sense in her, and sometimes, he thought she might even have a little sweetness. But she was very easily influenced by her brother.

"I told you not to tell," D.J. told her.

They stepped forward and she held out the hand she'd been hiding behind her back. "Here are the matches."

"Where did you get them?" Wade asked

Faith looked over at D.J., who shook his head at her. "I can't say. But we don't have any more."

At least it was a start.

"Thank you. Just so you know, your brother can't hurt you. If he does, there will be consequences."

D.J. balled his fists at his side. "You don't know anything."

"I know that your sister's afraid of you."

The twitching of the boy's cheek told Wade he was right. Especially as Faith's expression softened. Was there anyone this angry little boy didn't want to hurt?

Wade looked over Faith. "If he's mean to you, you tell me. I'll make it right."

Though Faith nodded, he could tell by her expression that she probably wouldn't confide in him. But he'd made the offer, and hopefully put the boy on notice that he wasn't going to be allowed to terrorize everyone anymore.

He gestured at the barn again. "Now go, get the tools you need, and get to work." The children remained where they were standing, and he didn't have time to spend more time convincing them to do the right thing. They would learn soon enough.

As he walked back toward the barn, he spotted Madison. He'd better go explain to her what had happened.

"Madison. Can we talk for a minute?"

For a moment, she looked uncertain, but then she nodded. "Of course. What's up?"

He explained what happened with her children, and he hated the disappointment on her face. She carried so many burdens, it seemed so unfair that what should have been the joys of her life was one of them.

"I'm so sorry," she said, raising a hand to her mouth. "I don't know what to do with them. It seems like everything I try only backfires. If you think chores will help, I'm all for it. It certainly couldn't make anything worse."

"Thank you. I was afraid I might have overstepped, but I honestly can't take it anymore. You deserve better than the way they treat you, and frankly, what I said about everyone in the family helping on the farm, that's how the farm works. It isn't fair that they get to lay around all day when everyone else is working so hard."

She nodded. "I've asked him to help, but they don't listen."

She glanced over to where the children were sitting in the grass. "If you can get them to listen, I'm all for it. I don't know what else to do."

A sad look crossed her face, and she shook her head. "Does that make me a bad mom? I do love them, and I want the best for them. I just can't figure out what I'm doing wrong."

He wanted to take her in his arms again, the way he had earlier. But he'd crossed a lot of lines with that conversation, and he didn't want to go there again.

"No, it makes you human. I don't have all the answers. I don't know if my idea will work. But it's a start."

She nodded. "You're right. I really appreciate the way you're investing yourself in my family. I know you don't have to do it, but I'm grateful you are."

He and Madison went to work on the backroom project and, as he'd suspected, Madison quickly set the room to rights. She had a knack for keeping things organized, and he liked how easily she did the job without much direction. When he was finished with what he needed to do, he went over to her. "I think that's good for now. I'll have you get back on it tomorrow. But for today, I'd like to finish teaching your children a lesson."

They walked back outside, where the children were still sitting where they been left on the lawn. Wade walked over to them, Madison trailing behind.

"I see you didn't get your job done," he said.

D.J. stared at him like he was an idiot, but Faith looked scared. Perhaps for his next task, he would separate them, giving Faith the chance to prove herself and also to receive a reward.

"Well that's too bad. Your mom and I are going out for ice cream, but it seems you won't be joining us."

The children looked nonplussed. All right then. That was

their choice.

"I expect your chores to be done when we get back," he said. "Or else there will be other consequences."

He hadn't thought of what those consequences might be, but surely they would be motivating.

They went into the house, and he let Enid know the plan.

A wicked gleam filled her eyes. "It's about time someone did something about those lazy children of yours, Madison."

Privately, he'd thought the same thing, but hadn't wanted to say so out of fear of offending Madison.

"I did so want great grandchildren to spoil, but those two are already spoiled beyond belief. I know you did the best you could, that's what Layla is always reminding me anyway. About everyone. But you're here now, and I think you're learning a little sense."

He glanced over at Madison, hoping she wasn't too offended by Enid's words. Sometimes the old woman spoke a little too harshly, thinking she was being helpful, but ended up offending others.

"I know," Madison said, sighing. "I tried, but there were so many things their father and I disagreed on. Dave wanted his children to have the best of everything, and I never fought him on it. I shouldn't have tried so hard to make my children's lives easy. Now that it's hard, they don't know what to do."

Enid nodded. "Yes, but they're young. They can learn. I also don't think they've been here long enough without gluten to have a chance for it all work out of their system. I know no one believes me when I say that gluten is the source of all unhappiness in the world, but I'm telling you. If everyone in the world would just stop eating gluten, we wouldn't have any problems."

Though most people thought Enid was crazy, Wade often thought she did have a point. Maybe not so much about the gluten, but he had noticed that since coming here and spending time with the Bigbys, eating more nutritious food, his general health and outlook on life had improved. Maybe it wasn't a scientific study, but he'd learned a lot in terms of how eating healthy food, straight from the farm, made him feel better.

"I'll admit to a weak moment at the Gas N' Shop the other day," Madison said, sighing. "We might have indulged in some junk food."

Enid jumped up. "I knew it. No wonder they've been particularly unruly lately. You cannot give into temptation."

Wade reached into his pocket, feeling the matches he'd taken from the children. They proudly bore the Gas N' Shop logo, so during that trip, they'd probably pilfered them. But he'd gotten the kids in enough trouble. He decided not to bring this up. Not this time.

"All right, you've convinced me." Then Madison turned and looked at Wade. "So, does this mean we can't go for ice cream? I was kind of looking forward to it."

Enid grinned. "There's no gluten in ice cream, at least not the flavors I like at Lik's. And, they have a special one, just for people like me who have to watch their sugars."

"I'll bring you back some," he told Enid, smiling at her. "But you have to promise me to eat it all in front of the children, enjoying every moment of it."

At Enid's excited cackle, he knew the older woman would be all too happy to participate in his plan. "I like how you think. I'll be glad to help."

He looked around the room. "Where's Hope? I was thinking we would take her, too."

Enid shook her head. "Napping. You two go on and have ice cream, and I'll share mine with Hope when you get back. I'm sure it will drive the other two crazy to see the baby getting ice cream when they can't have any."

CHAPTER 5

espite Madison's time in Arcadia Valley, she hadn't spent much time in the town itself. Her outings were limited to church, and the occasional stop at Gas N' Shop. Of course, after today's fiasco, that wasn't likely to happen either. Maybe Gram was right. Maybe all the junk food the kids liked was messing with their brains.

She certainly felt better eating healthier foods, even though at first the taste was hard to get used to. But now, she was starting to enjoy Gram's weird concoctions. And, though no one would ever call her skinny, she'd definitely lost some weight. Physically, she felt a lot better than she had before getting pregnant with Hope. As much as she hated to admit it, the snack cake that had looked so good at the Gas N' Shop had actually given her a stomach ache.

Walking through downtown Arcadia Valley, she appreciated the quaint shops and charming storefronts. In her previous life, she would have enjoyed buying things from each of them. But what would it have gotten her? Yes, there'd been a time when she could have passed by those cute little places and purchased whatever she'd wanted. But what did she have to show for all those purchases now?

So much of what she'd tried to sell had been deemed worthless, and at most, she'd gotten pennies on the dollar for what she paid for it. And none of that stuff had made her any happier. But as she paused by one of the shop windows, she couldn't help admiring a beautiful necklace on display.

"Facets has some nice stuff, don't they?" Wade asked.

She nodded, then turned away. "I had to sell all my jewelry to pay for things when Dave left. It's funny, though, I don't really miss any of it. I was just thinking how I'd had so many things that I'd wasted money on and ended up being useless. I'm amazed at the value we put on things that end up not being very valuable."

The expression on his face was warm, intelligent. Like he saw her that way as well. Dave used to tell her that it was a good thing she'd been so pretty, because he'd never thought she'd been very smart. She supposed if that was all he valued in her, it was no wonder he'd left when she gained weight.

But that was her old life and, as she caught her reflection in one of the shop windows, she didn't recognize the woman from that life anymore. Her highlights had grown out, and the usual sleek cut of her hairstyle had long lost its shape. Instead, her shaggy hair was back in a ponytail, and rather than wearing the latest fashions, she wore a pair of work pants and an old T-shirt she'd purchased at a thrift store. It hadn't even occurred to her to change clothes before they'd gone out for ice cream.

The old Madison would have been horrified at such a thought, but it felt good to be free of having such expectations on herself. She no longer needed the external approval she once so desperately sought.

She brushed a stray hair back behind her ear and turned to Wade. "So where is this ice cream place?"

He pointed at a cute little storefront with a yellow awning and seating outside. "Lik's just opened recently. I always thought this place could use a good old-fashioned ice cream parlor, and I appreciate their commitment to using fresh, local ingredients, and making their ice cream in store daily. It reminds me of summertime as a kid, when we would all sit in the backyard, and make our own ice cream. Their vanilla flavor tastes just like that."

His enthusiasm made her smile. Especially his mention of vanilla ice cream. It was nice to know that some people still liked the simple things. A few months ago, she would have been all about the latest wild and trendy flavors. But now, hearing the nostalgia and his voice about plain old vanilla ice cream, she had to agree. Sometimes the world was focused so much on new and better that they missed the simple pleasures of a classic.

"That sounds delicious. I'm a big fan of vanilla ice cream myself."

He looked over at her. "Not chocolate? I thought all women loved chocolate."

Madison smiled. "I wouldn't say no to chocolate, but I was just thinking about how we underestimate the choice of simplicity in the classics."

He nodded. "It's why I came back here. Being in the rat race nearly killed me. Don't get me wrong, my health is fine. On the outside, my life was perfect. But inside, I was a mess. I know people think I'm crazy, living the way I do, but I think a lot of the trappings of wealth only serve to confuse a person. I needed more from life than what materialism could give me."

She liked the philosophical way he spoke. In a way, it was the genuine version of Dave's words. Wade wasn't using his rejection of materialism as an excuse for his bad behavior, rather it truly seemed to be a life-changing event in his life.

In some ways, Dave's rejection of materialism was still a sign of his lust for material goods. Otherwise, he would have brought his wife and family with him on the journey. He wouldn't have given someone such a shallow excuse for the changes in his life. If he truly wanted to reject materialism, then he also would have rejected the idea of needing the perfect wife. Wouldn't he?

It was too bad Dave sought enlightenment from a pretty yoga instructor. Reliance on those outward things would only lead to more misery in the end. How could they not, when they were temporary?

She stole another glance at Wade, wondering what he looked like underneath the shaggy hair cut and overgrown beard. She'd once likened him to a homeless man, and the children used his appearance as a way to justify their mistreatment of him. Oddly enough, she found more to respect about Wade than she did about Dave.

And it wasn't just the fact that Dave had hurt her and made her life very difficult. Now, she struggled to think of what she had genuinely liked about her ex-husband.

They walked into the ice cream shop, and there was only one remaining table. Wade gestured to it. "Why don't you save us a spot, and I'll get the ice cream? Unless you want to go scope out the flavors? In which case I'll save the table, you go look, then come back and tell me what you want." He grinned. "This place gets busy, and I don't want to miss out on having a seat."

She glanced over at the counter. Tempting to try them all, or to find an exotic flavor, but she shook her head. "I believe I'll have the vanilla," she said.

Wade grinned. "After talking about it, that's what I want, too."

She reached for her purse, but Wade shook his head. "No, please. Let it be my treat. I know how hard you've been working, and while ice cream seems like a very small reward, I do want to show my appreciation for you. You're one of the best workers I've ever worked with, and I want you to know how thankful I am for you."

His praise warmed her. Especially after Dave's taunts about the fact that she'd never had a job, and probably wouldn't be able to handle one. A year ago, she'd have never imagined that she'd have been able to do such physical labor, but here she was.

"Thank you. That means a lot. I've been trying hard to do a good job, so I'm glad to hear that I'm succeeding."

"Definitely. I wish more people had your work ethic."

He went to get the ice cream, and she couldn't help noticing the confidence in his walk, and the way some of the people in the shop greeted him, like an old friend. No one shied away from him because of his appearance, because they all knew what a good heart he had. At least that's what she figured. Because that's what she thought of him.

He laughed at something the woman at the counter said, and she had to admit, even though no one would be so bold as to call him classically handsome, there was something very attractive about him. That was the thing about inner beauty. When it radiated from the inside, it made the outside so much more appealing.

Wade returned, carrying three ice cream cups.

"Three? I know you were going to bring some for Gram, but won't it melt if you get it now?"

He grinned. "I know we were both set on vanilla, but I'd forgotten that they'd bought some of Allie's lavender to make a lavender ice cream. I thought we owed it to her to at least try it."

Because so much of Bigby Farm was devoted to Allie's lavender operation, Madison had tried everything in lavender. Lavender soap, lavender candles, lavender tea, lavender everything. But ice cream?

He must've seen the look on her face, because he dipped a spoon in the cup. "It's just a taste. Surely you've had worse things at Enid's than lavender ice cream."

Madison grinned. "You mean like that weird rutabaga juice that she makes us all drink?"

He chuckled. "If you can drink that stuff, you can drink anything. Besides, this isn't anywhere close to it." He put a spoonful of ice cream in his mouth, and she watched as he seemed to be very intently exploring the flavor.

"Well?" She studied the expression on his face to see if it was pleasurable or not.

He smiled at her. "It's delicious. Just like the name."

"What's the name?"

"Lavender romance."

She stared at him for a moment. "Lavender romance? That's a weird name for ice cream. How can you say it tastes just like the name? I know what lavender tastes like, but romance?"

He shook his head slowly. "Surely romance has a flavor. Sweet, adventurous, refreshing, and comforting, all at the same time. Though one bite satisfies you, it lingers in your memory, making you want more."

All that from a simple bite of ice cream? The twinkle in his eyes made her wonder if he was teasing her, or maybe even flirting. He'd called her beautiful earlier, and she hadn't known what to do with that, nor did she know what to do with these ideas he was putting in her head.

"Those all sound like lovely things, but it's been a long time since I've thought of romance. So long that I don't even remember what it's like."

He pushed the cup of ice cream in her direction. "Then remember. I know you've been hurt, and you probably still miss your husband, but it doesn't do you any good to remain stuck in the past."

As she looked down at the cup of ice cream, she tried to find a diplomatic way of telling him how she really felt. That it had been so long since she and Dave had shared any kind of connection, she felt no nostalgia for such things. Instead, she took a bite.

It was every bit as delicious as Wade had said. And, as she let the flavors roll around on her tongue, she agreed with his description. Except for the romance part.

She swallowed the ice cream and looked up at him. "I do like it. But I don't know what's romantic about it. I never had that with Dave. In a way, life with him was like those old worn-out slippers with a little hole in the toe, and smell kind of funny, but you don't want to throw them away because they're broken in so well."

Wade gave her an encouraging look that didn't make her feel as pathetic as she thought she sounded in describing her old life.

"That's not a way to live your life," she said. "Obviously, Dave felt the same way, because he threw the slippers away. I clung to them, and I did my best to try to repair them, but they never smelled any better."

Wade chuckled, like he knew what she meant, and it comforted her to know he didn't think she was crazy.

She took another bite of the ice cream. "I think what attracted me to Dave in the beginning was the forbidden nature of our relationship. My mother had sheltered me so much that being with Dave gave me freedom I never had. But the more I think about my feelings for him, the more I think they were mostly about lust."

Way TMI, but his idealized version of romance bore no resemblance to her experience. "We got married because I was pregnant. We thought we were doing the right thing, and I do believe it was. But we were too busy following that passion to think about laying a foundation for when I wasn't some cute little thing and our lives became ordinary."

Wade gave her the same look he always gave her when he thought she was putting herself down, but she shook her head at him and reached for the cup of vanilla ice cream.

"The lavender is lovely," she said. "But at the very core, it's just plain vanilla. When the lavender fades, or it's out of season, this is what you have left. And if you don't appreciate it from the very beginning, how do you appreciate it later?"

Wade took her hand. "Maybe that's what your relationship with Dave was, not appreciating the vanilla. But you know better now, and you can make different choices."

She looked down at the large tanned hand covering hers. "I think that's the lure of the lavender talking. That fresh and exotic taste, leading to wanting to chase other new and exciting things. I don't have that in me anymore."

He gave her a smile that warmed her deep within her soul. "You're really wise," he said. "I suspect that comes from a lot of long, hard experience."

She looked down at her ice cream. "Unfortunately, I had to lose everything to come to that realization. And yet, coming to Bigby Farm, I've gained so much more." Then she took another bite of the ice cream. "I just wish I could figure out how to get my kids to understand that. I wish Dave hadn't skipped town so that he could face it. And maybe that's why he ran off like that. He was too weak, too scared, to face the reality of what he was doing."

Wade regarded her with an intensity that made her slightly uncomfortable. "His weakness has nothing to do with you, you know that, right?"

The ice cream sat funny in her stomach. It had tasted good at first, still did, but after so long without sugar, the sweetness was too much.

"We should go," she said.

"I thought you were critical of people who ran."

He was right. Everyone had to confront the truth some-time. Even though Dave had gone halfway across the world, he would still have to face what he'd done. There would be a reckoning, and the longer he waited, the worse it would be.

"Yes. Intellectually, I know that. But deep in my heart, I still wonder what I had done wrong."

"Do you still love him?"

She shrugged. "I'm not sure I could use that word to describe our relationship or my feelings for him. To be honest, the past few years of our marriage, we were both just going through the motions. I'm mostly just sad that we let our marriage degenerate so far. No one tells you that after the puppy dog phase of love, marriage is a lot of work. Taking the time to get to know each other, finding out each other's needs, and connecting on a real level."

He gestured at her unfinished bowl of ice cream. "It's going to melt."

"I hate for food to go to waste, but it's too sweet. Before coming here, I would have devoured it with no problem. But I think Gram's war on sugar has been won with me. I don't want it anymore."

"There are worse things. I may not be as militant about it as your grandmother, but I agree with her ideas about sugar. We eat entirely too much, and it takes a toll on our health."

"One more thing my kids don't understand."

He reached out and took her hands again. "They will. I know you're discouraged, and it feels like everything is against you, but in the long run, I think your kids are going to see what a strong mother they have, and they will appre-ciate the love you've given them."

She hoped so, too, but right now, with her son's voice in

the back of her head, taunting her for being fat, she couldn't see past it.

"You're a good woman," Wade continued. "Your husband was too much of a fool to see it. But I believe, with all the good people around him, your son will eventually get there."

She glanced at the clock. They'd been sitting here for over an hour. Though it was nice to have a break, she also didn't want to take advantage of her family. Especially given the state of her children's attitudes right now.

They gathered their things, and Wade went to get some ice cream to go for Gram. He came away with a large container, smiling as he sheepishly explained that he thought everyone should get a taste of lavender romance.

The way he said it—lavender romance—sent chills up and down her spine. Was this the start of romance? She already knew that he was attracted to her, he'd said as much earlier. And his encouraging words and touches, while not inappropriate, made her wonder if perhaps they were a hint of something more.

When they got back to the house, Gram was sitting on the porch with Hope. The little girl was snuggled up against her, and Gram was fixing her hair. It might have seemed like a little thing, but Madison's heart melted at the sight. The kids had never had family to pour into them like that.

Her mom still lived in the house where she grew up in Southern California, too far from Silicon Valley for more than the occasional phone call, video chat, and birthday card. They weren't close, and her children really didn't know their grandmother. Hope might have met her once, but that was all. Dave's parents, who'd been older when they'd had him to begin with, had passed when the older children were young.

Though D.J. and Faith might not appreciate their circumstances, at least Hope would understand what a gift it was to be part of such a large, loving family.

When she got out of the car, Hope jumped up and ran to her. "Mama."

Madison scooped her little girl up in her arms and held her tight, breathing in her baby scent. She'd obviously been given a bath, which meant she'd probably wet the bed during her nap again. But Gram never seemed to condemn Madison for it or accuse her of being a bad mother the way others did. She kissed the top of her little girl's head, and Hope wiggled to be free.

"Down."

She let the little girl go, and Hope ran back to Gram. "More pretty."

Gram chuckled and patted her lap. "Well sit down, and don't wiggle."

Wade joined her, holding up the ice cream. "They had some made with Allie's lavender, so I had to bring some back for everyone to try."

The announcement of ice cream seemed to bring everyone out from the woodwork. Allie came from around the side of the house, wiping her hands on her pants. "What's this about lavender ice cream?"

"Remember that ice cream place in town? I told you they bought some of your lavender at the farmers' market because they wanted to try making ice cream from it. It's quite good," Wade said.

Allie's husband, Cole, came around the side of the house. "Did someone say lavender ice cream?"

Which led to Caroline and Hayden hot on his heels.

Madison had always thought that having a large family would feel too constricting and confining. But she loved how they all came together, especially when it came to sharing something delicious. Plus, like everyone else on the farm, they were restricted by Gram's strict no sugar policy. Granted, that's what Allie liked anyway, but all the siblings tended to have their own guilty pleasures when it came to food. They might have their own houses now, but it was amazing how the family still seemed to come together for most meals.

And then, another couple came around the side of the house, holding hands and laughing. She hadn't met Andrew and Layla yet because they had been gone when she arrived, but she knew them from their picture.

"Layla. Andrew. Come meet Madison." Allie's voice was dripping with excitement, and Madison smiled. Their correspondence over email had made them both hope that they would become great friends. Allie was even better in person.

At Layla's warm smile, Madison knew she would find another good friend.

After introductions and hugs were exchanged, Wade came out of the house, carrying bowls and spoons. She hadn't noticed him going to get them, because she'd been too busy meeting the rest of her family. But it was nice of Wade to find a way to be helpful.

Her children, however, were nowhere to be seen.

She turned to Gram. "You haven't seen D.J. and Faith, have you?"

Gram shook her head.

"Maybe they decided to do the right thing and clean out the chicken coop like they were asked," Wade said. "It would be nice for them to try the ice cream, too."

Allie shook her head. "I doubt it."

Madison let out a long sigh. "I'll go look for them."

Even though she appreciated everyone's concern, it made her feel bad to hear all the voices chorusing their willingness to join in. It wasn't like her children were actually missing. They were just getting into trouble—again.

CHAPTER 6

*W*ade hated for Madison to have to leave her cousins, especially when she'd finally gotten the chance to meet Andrew and Layla. It hardly seemed fair, stealing the obvious joy written all over her face. He was glad he'd been able to take her out for ice cream, giving her a break from the stresses of her life. She carried so much on her shoulders, and he hated that she had to bear them all alone. Giving the kids the benefit of the doubt, he went by the chicken coop, just in case they decided to do their job.

They clearly hadn't even been there.

He walked around to the hay barn, one of the places he'd seen them playing. They seemed to like it in there, even though D.J. also was constantly complaining about how filthy it was.

Sure enough, that's where he found them. D.J. was throwing eggs against one of the walls.

"What are you doing?" As he came toward them, the kids stopped, but D.J. looked at him with the same defiant expression he'd worn when Wade had caught him playing with matches.

"Just trying to have a little fun," D.J. said.

"That's not fun, not when those eggs are valuable to this farm. Not only is that what we eat, but we sell the extras at the farmers' market to bring in extra money."

D.J. glared at him. "Eggs are cheap. I don't know what you're so worried about."

Wade glanced at the damage the kids had done. "Good. Then you will pay for every broken egg. How many were there?"

The kids stared at him blankly.

"How are we supposed to do that? We don't have any money," D.J. said.

"I thought you said eggs were cheap."

D.J. rolled his eyes. "For adults who have money. If you've got so much money, then you pay for them."

He'd never met a kid with such a big chip on his shoulder before. Then again, he'd never met a kid whose dad just disappeared right after Christmas. At least Andrew was home now. Maybe Andrew could give them some insight as to how to help this little boy. D.J.'s father wasn't dead, but he might as well be. It was the same level of sudden loss, with no explanation.

"I'm also going to expect you to clean up this mess. All these broken eggs will attract critters, and we don't want any in the barn."

D.J. rolled his eyes again. "The place is already filthy. What does it matter if there's a few more eggs laying around."

A lot, but the boy had already proven to be unreasonable, and wasn't likely to understand his explanation. Faith, though, had a softness to her posture that indicated she was a little more willing to listen to reason.

He turned to her. "How many eggs did you guys use?"

She pointed to the crate where they kept the eggs to take to the farmers' market. It was empty. A week's worth of eggs, and they were all gone. The worst part was, this wasn't just about them and their livelihood, but about customers who counted on them for healthy, nutritious eggs.

"You guys broke all those eggs?" Wade asked.

Faith nodded. "And the ones we took out of the coop. I was going to do what you said, but then D.J. got the idea to play a game with the eggs. When we ran out, we used the rest in the barn. He was trying to do it like this artist we saw on TV."

"Shut up, tattletale. This is why I don't include you in any of my games. You don't know anything about being fun. You're so afraid of getting in trouble. What's he going to do to you?" D.J. asked.

Shadows filled the end of the barn. Madison stepped forward. "Whatever he wants," she said in a tone that made Wade grateful he wasn't the one being scolded. "I don't even know how to express my sorrow at what just happened here."

She looked over at Wade. "Did they really break all of the eggs?"

He nodded. "I'm afraid so."

As Enid entered the barn, he could see the great dismay on her face. It was said that she was pretty hard on her kids growing up, and though she'd definitely developed a softer side over the years, how was she going to react?

"Do you have any idea what you've done?" Enid asked.

The kids stared at her with the same blank expressions they always wore when anyone asked anything of them.

"Well," she said. "You're going to. You'll go with Wade tomorrow to the farmers' market, and whenever a customer comes and asks where their eggs are, you're going to tell them that you destroyed them. I want you to look each one of them in the eye and see their reaction to what you've done. Those are our friends and neighbors, and they're counting on us. You get to let them know that you've let them down."

"What do I care if some people don't get the eggs they ordered? Eggs are disgusting. We eat too many of them." The boy's expression was absolutely unrepentant. Like he truly didn't care about others.

"I'm sure they'll tell you all about it when you explain you don't have their eggs," Enid said, giving him a firm look. "You make sure you two get this place cleaned up. We don't want any varmints to get in here."

"That's exactly what I said," Wade told her. "They don't seem to understand the consequences of animals getting attracted to the barn."

"It's filthy," D.J. said. "A little more won't make any difference."

Enid grinned. "Good. Messes bother you. That's real good. Once you clean up in here, you can sweep the whole barn out, and then, I think this place could use a good scrubbing."

She turned to Madison. "What do you think? I'm sure there are places you're supposed to clean that you haven't gotten to yet. Your son is really concerned with cleaning, so you can give him all your cleaning duties. Faith will help him."

D.J. gave the same disgusted look he always did when asked to do something. So far, he hadn't responded to anyone positively, but maybe Enid had the magic touch. Someone had to be able to get through to this boy. Even though Madison said there was no way of reaching her ex, it was tempting to see if he could find a way to contact the boy's father to talk some sense into him.

But as he remembered the tortured expression on Madison's face as she talked about her ex, he wasn't sure if that would create more problems than it solved. Given the boy's propensity for lying, and the fact that he already quoted his father ad nauseum, the apple probably didn't fall far from the tree. What idiotic excuse would he have for abandoning his children like that?

He glanced over at Madison, who looked utterly exhausted. Maybe looking up her ex wasn't the answer. But something had to be done to help her with this out of control kid.

THEY WENT BACK to the back porch and Layla served the lavender ice cream. Even though Madison had already had her fill, she took the ice cream and made a big show of eating it with the others. Not long after, D.J. and Faith wandered out of the barn.

"Where's ours?" D.J. asked.

Gram shrugged. "Treats are only for those who do their work. You were given a number of chores today and didn't do them."

"That's not fair." D.J. stomped the ground.

"It is fair," Madison said. "Gram is right. We all did our work, and we've given you plenty of opportunity to do yours."

Wade made a big show of taking a large bite. "This is so good. Allie, I hope you work out a deal with them to supply more lavender. I think lavender ice cream is going to be the next big thing."

Allie took a bite of her ice cream. "I completely agree. Personally, I think we should use lavender for everything. But I just have to convince the rest of the world."

As each family member made a show of eating and enjoying the ice cream, D.J. and Faith grew angrier. Even though it was nice to get a response out of them, Madison wished it were something other than anger. It was always anger with them, and she'd love to hear the laughter and whoops of joy she'd once heard from all of her children.

"This is child abuse," D.J. said.

"No it's not," Madison said. "We gave you plenty of opportunities to enjoy ice cream with us. If you had made the right decision about doing your chores, you'd be joining us."

As D.J. scowled, Hope hobbled over to her. "Ice cream?"

Madison spooned some ice cream into the little girl's mouth and everyone seemed enraptured by the little girl enjoying a tasty treat. She hopped off her mother's lap, then wandered over to her grandmother, who gave her more.

"That's not fair. Hope didn't clean the chicken coop."

Madison smiled at her son. "No, she didn't. But she did help Gram in the garden earlier today, and she's been a good girl all day."

She smiled indulgently at her youngest daughter. "You helped Gram pick tomatoes, didn't you?"

"Ma-toes," Hope said, her face full of ice cream.

Gram grinned. "She sure did. And she helped me fold all the clean laundry. Hope is such a good helper."

Then she gave Hope another spoonful of ice cream.

D.J.'s face darkened and he stormed off. But Faith stood there, watching them.

"If I go do my share of the chores, can I have some ice cream later?" she asked.

The kids had been deprived of sweets for so long, and the two older children loved their sugar. Madison had hoped the original bribe would work, but maybe, now that they saw the reward, they'd be more likely to give in to their love of sweets.

She looked over at Wade. "What do you think? You're the one who set the requirement to begin with. I don't want to go against your wishes."

She liked the way Wade looked at Faith with tenderness. Sympathy. Like he was trying to understand what it was like to be a little girl whose life had changed so dramatically in such a short period of time.

"Clean up the chicken coop, and the mess in the barn, and if you get it done before supper time, you can have a little bit. But in the future, you'll do your chores the first time, without complaint, or you won't get the reward."

Faith nodded slowly, then said meekly, "I did tell him that throwing the eggs was a bad idea. But he doesn't listen to me."

"But you could have chosen not to go along with him," Madison said. "You could have chosen to do the chores, even though you would've had to do it by yourself, I'm sure Wade would have rewarded you for doing your brother's share on top of yours."

Wade nodded. "I don't expect you to do your brother's chores, and I don't want him forcing you into that position. But I definitely reward extra work. Who knows? If you were to do more chores than just what you were assigned, I might even give you some money."

Faith's face lit up. "Gram told me that there's a bookstore in town. I don't have many books, and all the ones Gram has are boring. Who is that Nancy Drew girl, anyway?"

She'd really gotten into the graphic novels, but they were expensive, and the waiting list at the library was always so long. They hadn't been to the library in Arcadia Valley yet, but at the wistful look on her daughter's face, Madison knew she needed to make the time to do so soon.

"It sounds like you have some real good motivation to get your work done," Wade said. "Do your best, and don't let your brother distract you, and it will all work out."

Faith turned and walked in the direction the chicken coop, and though Madison knew she should have said something more motherly and encouraging, she couldn't find the words.

She shook her head slowly as she looked up at her family. "I don't know what I'm doing wrong."

Layla sat next to her. "It sounds like D.J. is really grieving the loss of his father. But he doesn't know what to do with it, so he's acting out." She looked up at Andrew, who nodded, then joined them on the bench.

"Layla is absolutely right. It was a sudden loss for everyone, and as hard as it is, they need to accept a life without him."

Madison sighed. Hadn't she been trying to do that?

"They blame me."

Layla took her hand. "Of course they do. The person responsible isn't here to take responsibility, so it's no wonder that your son can't accept responsibility for his actions. He has the example of a man who won't do it either."

It felt good, having the support of so many people who loved her. But it didn't solve the problem at hand.

"What am I supposed to do about it?"

"One of my instructors specializes in adolescent psychology," Andrew said. "I can give you some ideas on general things, and managing grief, but Dr. Beard is an expert in adolescence, so I'm sure she will have ideas that I haven't thought of. D.J.'s at such a hard age, and since his brain hasn't fully developed yet, it's a lot harder for him to process the pain of an absent father."

Hayden and Caroline joined them. "I agree," Hayden said. "My parents divorced when I was a kid, and it was hard on me. My father was emotionally absent, but not so emotionally absent that I didn't at least hear something from him. I idolized my father, and it took meeting Caroline to understand how unhealthy it all was. Fortunately, as I understood more about what a healthy family dynamic was, and through a few counseling sessions, I was able to put my relationship with my father in proper perspective and realize that all of those failures I thought were mine were actually his. And that he wasn't capable of having the kind of relationship with me that I wanted with him."

Caroline walked over to Hayden and put her arms around him. "But, he is also working on it, and it's really wonderful that we've all learned to have healthier relationships with our parents."

The love in Hayden's eyes as he looked back at Caroline was apparent. For a moment, Madison envied them. She'd never had such a relationship with Dave. At least not that she could remember.

"And I have you to thank for that," Hayden said, pressing a kiss on top of Caroline's head before turning his attention back to Madison. "What your kids' father did to them makes him the worst kind of coward. They deserve better than that. One day, they'll realize it, and, hopefully, their hearts won't be too broken when they realize the man they idolized is nothing more than a big jerk. But with love, and therapy, they'll get through."

"I think therapy is good for everyone in a difficult situation," Andrew said. "I don't mean to be butting in where I'm unwelcome, so please know this is a suggestion made only in love. But you might consider going to one of the divorce support groups at church. It could help you to get to know the other women in your situation, meet other parents who are struggling with helping their children manage something similar. And, if my professor doesn't give you anything you find helpful, the people in the group might be able to suggest someone. Obviously, we're all going to do the best we can to love D.J. through this difficult time. But I do think having professional help will speed up the process."

"I'm not offended at all," Madison assured them. "I appre-

ciate it. To be honest, I'd really hoped to give the kids counseling. But that's hard to do on my budget."

As she looked at all the faces watching her, she realized
what her family must be thinking. "And no, that's not me
asking for more money. Just telling you the facts. Now that I
have money from working at the farm, I can start looking at
it, and seeing what I can find. We just went without for so
long that I'm trying to prioritize where to spend my money."

It helped that Gram refused to accept anything toward
household expenses, and that her cousins had vehemently
agreed. But the one bill she still had was her car payment. It
might seem too much of an extravagance to have her luxury
SUV, but when she'd tried trading it in for something cheaper,
they'd taken too much off the value because of the kid stains
in the interior for it to be worth it. She'd still be paying off the
SUV and another car. But, with the money she was making
working for Allie, she'd been able to catch up on payments,
and only had a few more to go before that loan was taken care
of. Then, she could put more toward the credit card bills Dave
had racked up, and slowly, she'd get out of this mess.

Hayden looked over at her. "Doesn't your ex have to pay
child support and alimony? Surely, with as long as you were
married, and the fact that your sole responsibility was
providing for the household, he should owe you alimony."

She tried not to laugh. "It's in the divorce decree. But just
because the divorce decree says he owes it doesn't mean he's
going to pay it. I know the courts can do things like garnish
wages and such, but when he doesn't have a job and has left
the country, it's hard to find him to get the money."

Hayden nodded slowly. "That does present a problem.
You don't mind if I look into it, do you?"

He could look all he wanted, but it didn't mean he was
going to find anything. The judge had even held Dave in

contempt of court, for not showing up to one of the hearings, then granted her the final decree and everything her lawyer asked for. He'd already been on his way to India then, so even contempt charges didn't mean a thing. And his lawyer, disgusted by it all, had agreed to everything. Apparently, Dave owed him money, too.

"If you're willing to look, I don't mind, but I'm not sure you'll find anything other than miles of debt."

Hayden nodded. "You'd be surprised. Even if he can't pay now, unless he goes to court to have it modified, he still owes you all that money. Hopefully, he'll return to the States someday, and he'll be forced to pay."

It all sounded good, but money wasn't what she wanted anymore. "I would just be happy if he would come back and talk to his son. I'm no longer mad about him betraying me. But the kids? How could he do that to his children? He owes them an explanation."

Wade muttered something under his breath, and Allie kicked him.

"What was that?" Madison turned to look at her cousin.

"Nothing," Allie said. "Wade was being inappropriate."

"It's not inappropriate to want to punch a guy for doing that to his wife and kids. Maybe violence isn't the answer, but I'd sure like to see him suffer for the way those kids have suffered."

Everyone murmured agreements, and Madison's heart did a funny leap at the thought of having so many people standing behind her.

The sky was slightly darkening as the sun went down, and the wind had picked up a bit.

Gram stood. "I know we all just had ice cream, but it's getting late and I should start supper. I'll heat up the soup I made earlier."

Allie looked over at Layla. "Soup? I thought we talked her out of that."

Gram paused at the back door. "No one talks me in or out of anything I don't want to do. You might not like my rutabaga soup, but it's good for the soul."

Everyone groaned except Wade. "I've got some venison steaks we can throw on the grill," he said. "I'd started defrosting three of them, thinking I would grill them all up tonight, then use the leftovers this week as lunches and such. But I don't mind bringing them over and we can all share."

Madison shook her head. "We can't eat your lunch. What will you have?"

He grinned. "You're just afraid of trying venison. I saw how you picked at your roast the other night. With the marinade I've had them in all day, these are going to taste like a million dollars. Trust me."

Layla gave her another warm squeeze. "It's hard to get used to, I know. I felt the same way when Andrew told me what we were eating. But I've done a lot of research on the health benefits of venison, and it's really a great meat for optimum nutrition. With the veggies from the garden, we can have a nice salad. So, try a few bites, and if you still don't like it, there's plenty of other food. Unless you'd rather just eat the rutabaga soup."

Madison wasn't sure which one would make her gag more, but they were right. Every time Wade brought them over some venison, she'd find a convenient excuse not to eat it. But choosing between rutabaga soup and venison, though she was in no danger of starvation, her stomach rumbled at the thought of going without.

"All right," she said. "I'll give it a try."

The way he looked at her made her feel special, like she mattered to him. And being here, with her new family, and

Wade, she was starting to realize that she truly had a place where she belonged. Something she'd never felt before.

Wade left to get the steaks, and Madison went to check on her daughter, who was diligently working on the chicken coop.

"Nice work," Madison said. "I can see you'll be really earning that ice cream tonight. Where's your brother?"

She shrugged, but something in her body language told Madison that she knew exactly where he was.

"Where is he?"

"I don't know," she said. "I told him he should help me, but he ran off. But I heard what Uncle Hayden said about dad being a coward."

She hadn't realized the children had overheard. Though she usually tried protecting them from hearing the negative things about their father, maybe this time it wasn't a bad thing. They could see that their father wasn't the hero the kids made him out to be.

Faith looked at the ground, then looked up at her. "It really upset D.J. He doesn't like hearing bad things about Dad, even if they're true."

This was the first time Faith had been willing to admit, even in a small way, that maybe their dad wasn't so perfect. Madison put her arm around her daughter.

"I wish you'd talk to me about these things and not let them fester. I know you guys think I'm the enemy, but I'm here for you."

Her daughter nodded slowly. "It's just because D.J.'s sad about Dad being gone. I am, too. Why didn't he love us enough to stay? Or even let us visit on the weekend's like Kinley's dad?"

And there was the crux of her children's pain.

"Because there's something wrong with him, not you," Madison said, giving her daughter another squeeze.

"I know you think you did something wrong, or aren't enough in some way for him, but you have to understand, none of this is your fault."

Faith pulled away and looked up at her. "So it's yours? Why don't you just get skinny again so he'll take us all back?"

Madison shook her head. "Even if I was skinny, I wouldn't want him back. I know you guys hate it here, but being on the farm, away from the things we were used to, I've learned a lot. I know I am a smart, capable woman, and I can do a lot of things I never thought I could, no matter what size I am. I'm surrounded by family who love and accept me for who I am. And Faith, that's what I want for you. You deserve to be loved, no matter what, without having to be perfect. Love isn't about being perfect. Love is about accepting what's wrong with a person and choosing to love them anyway. I love you like that, and if your father can't, that's his problem, not yours."

As Faith started to cry, Madison took her into her arms, repeating over and over how much she loved her little girl.

After a few moments, Faith looked up. "But I've been so bad lately."

"And I haven't stopped loving you. I never will."

As she gave her daughter a final hug, she looked in the direction Wade had gone.

All those things she'd described to her daughter about love, she'd seen it modeled by Wade. After today's events, there were... sparks... that she—No. Madison shook her head as she gave her daughter another hug. Her focus needed to be on her kids. Not on the first man to strike her fancy in a long time.

But still, she'd be lying if she said his comments about her weight, and liking her for who she was, hadn't done something to her heart she'd never experienced before.

CHAPTER 7

*N*ormally, Wade let one of the other farm workers handle things at the farmers' market. But since Enid had insisted on going and bringing D.J. and Faith to apologize to every one of their customers for the egg incident, he felt he needed to be there to supervise. Not just the kids. Sometimes, Enid and her unconventional ways got her in trouble.

Wade sent out a silent plea that God would work in the kids today. Maybe not so much transform them, but at least get them to behave. He'd run out of options and didn't know what else to do. Andrew's professor recommended a therapist for D.J., but his schedule didn't have any openings, and though Faith's attitude had improved considerably, D.J. was still as sullen as ever. Even now, he sat in a chair by the stand, scowling.

Enid must have noticed the boy's attitude, because she walked over to him. "None of that. We have to smile and make our customers think they're welcome, not scare them off."

Wade tried not to laugh. Enid had scared off plenty of customers in her day.

D.J. glared at her. "It wasn't my idea to be here."

"I guess you should have thought of that when you ruined the eggs for my customers. Maybe, in the future, you'll have better ideas." Enid gave him a sharp look, but then she softened. "You're a smart boy, and if you would just use those smarts for good, you'd really make something of yourself."

D.J. stood. "I am going to make something of myself. Just give me a computer, and I'll make millions."

"Is that so?" Enid turned to Wade. "You never told that boy what you used to do for a living, did you?"

Wade shook his head. He didn't like talking about those days, especially because, while it would probably impress the boy, he wouldn't understand why Wade had given it up.

"I did some programming," Wade said. "Taught myself on a computer I built myself when I was about your age."

Then he had an idea. So simple, he should have thought of it before, but he generally closed himself to any ideas relating to his old work.

"I'll tell you what. You like computers so much, I'll give you one of mine."

For a moment, D.J.'s eyes widened, but the scowl quickly returned. "You're going to make me earn it, aren't you?"

"Nothing in this world comes for free, and even if it seems like it is, there's something you have to do in return. In your case, I want a change in attitude. Your dad is gone, and it stinks, I get that. But you have to stop treating everyone like it's their fault. You show a little respect, and that computer is all yours. You probably already know a lot of programming, but I'd be willing to teach you what I know."

Enid was nodding approvingly, and even Faith had come around to listen to the conversation.

"That one will cost you. You do all your chores, without

complaint, and then you'll get a lesson. But the first time I hear or see attitude from you, no lesson that day. And if I see it a second time, you lose computer privileges for the day."

For a kid who'd been deprived of his beloved computers for so long, it was a good deal. But D.J. shook his head. "It's just a trick to get me to do what you want me to do. How do I even know you know anything about computers?"

Before he could answer, Josh Patton, the youth pastor at Arcadia Valley community church, approached.

"Enid. Nice to see you out. We usually don't get the pleasure at the farmers' market."

Enid made a noise. "They say I scare away the customers. But my great-grandson is even scarier. Then people will take a look at Wade, and I'm sure they'll go running. The only hope is my pretty little great-granddaughter, who has enough beauty to make up for us all."

Josh chuckled. "Wade definitely won't win any beauty prizes with that ugly beard of his, but he is the smartest computer guy I know. We couldn't afford any of the expensive check-in systems for child care at our church, so Wade built one for us from scratch. And, he updated all our other computer systems so that everything works amazingly well. We had some guy visiting from out of state, and he tried hiring Wade to do the same for his church, but Wade wouldn't do it. Said he had too much going on here."

He'd asked Josh not to say anything, because he didn't like people knowing all the things he did to help others. But looking at the awe in D.J.'s face made him not mind so much. Especially because Josh had made it clear that Wade wasn't in it for the money.

"Why wouldn't you go work for that guy?" D.J. asked. "Then you wouldn't be homeless, and you could contribute to society."

Wade shrugged. "As I told you before, I'm not homeless. I

own the house that Allie and Cole live in, but I rent it to them, because I prefer living in my tiny house. As for having a job and contributing to society, I work for Bigby Farm, and I love my job. Maybe that isn't as glamorous as being a computer programmer, but I wouldn't live my life any other way. Still, if being a computer programmer is your dream, I'd be happy to teach you what I know."

For a moment, Wade thought D.J. was going to agree. The little boy's eyes lit up in and he looked almost excited. But then a frown marred his features.

"You're just being nice to me because you like my mom. My dad says that some guys have a thing for fatties, and I guess you're one of them."

If another man had said that to him, Wade would've had no problem punching him. But this was a boy, a hurting child, and he didn't know what he was saying.

But Josh stared at D.J. "I don't know who your dad is, but if he were any kind of a man, he wouldn't say such things to his son."

D.J. glared at him. "I didn't ask you. It's not my dad's fault the ladies love him. When I grow up, I'm going to be just like him."

Enid turned and looked at him. "Is that so? You're going to abandon your wife and children? You keep telling everyone how great your dad is, but in my eighty plus years of living, I've never heard of such a scoundrel."

"My dad loves me. I just know that one day soon, he'll be coming for me. And then I can get out of this horrible place, and never have to see any of you people again."

The little boy's face had turned red, and he looked like he was about to cry, showing them all the vulnerability of a child who'd been abandoned but didn't want to admit to it.

Faith came around the table and put her arm around her brother. "You keep saying that, but he never comes. Every time you get the chance to be on Aunt Allie's iPad with Wi-Fi, you send him an email, but he never answers. His phone number belongs to someone else now, and he forgot all of our birthdays."

D.J. turned and shoved his sister to the ground, then took off running. Faith started to cry, and Wade was torn as to what to do.

"I'll go after them," Josh said. "It sounds like you've already been dealing with him, so maybe having another man talking to him will help."

"Thanks," Wade said to Josh, then he knelt beside the little girl. "Are you okay?"

Faith nodded, and her eyes were red and puffy from crying. He could see a dribble of snot running from her nose, so he reached into his pocket for a napkin that he'd taken earlier when he'd gotten coffee and handed it to her. "Here."

"I keep thinking about what Mom said the other day, about how people who really love you are there for you. I know D.J. says that Dad was wonderful, but he missed my birthday party the past three years. He was always busy with work. He sent balloons to school, but I don't even like balloons. I just wanted my dad to come have lunch with me, like my mom did."

She blew her nose and looked over at him. "We've been really mean to you, but you keep being nice to us. You were even trying to help D.J. learn computer stuff so he can be rich and famous just like dad told him he would be. I guess that means you love us more than our dad does, doesn't it?"

The longing in her eyes made him want to weep. He held out his arms to her. "I can't say for sure that I know anything about your dad. But you're right. If I had a little girl like you, I would be there for everything."

She breached the distance between them, and hugged him tight. "I'm sorry we've been so mean to you," she said.

"I forgive you." He gave her another squeeze, then helped her to her feet. "It looks like we've got some customers coming, so maybe later, we can talk about this some more. Just remember, I'm always here if you need me."

Charlotte Delis approached with her little girl, Elena. If he remembered correctly, Elena was near Faith's age. They went to a different church, and school hadn't started yet, so Faith hadn't had a chance to meet the Delis girl.

Wade smiled at Charlotte. "Hello Charlotte. Elena. There's someone I'd like you to meet."

He gave Faith a little nudge. "This is Faith. She's Enid's great-granddaughter, and she's come to live with Enid. She hasn't had a chance to make many friends yet, so I thought you'd like to meet her."

Elena's eyes grew as wide as the pumpkins they sold in the fall. "You get to live on Bigby Farm?"

Faith nodded but didn't speak. She half hid behind Wade, shielding herself in an unfamiliar situation.

"That's so cool. Imagine being around all those animals. And the garden." Elena looked up at Charlotte. "You've always said how much you admired the garden at Bigby Farm."

Charlotte smiled affectionately at the little girl. "Yes, I have. It's so nice to see another girl your age with similar interests. Do you like animals, Faith?"

Though Faith remain hidden behind Wade, she nodded. "Since Wade is the manager, he makes me do chores, to help with the animals."

"I help out with the chores at our house, too," Elena said.

"I'm sure my brother would let you do his share. He'd rather be stuck in his room on the computer. But I've always wanted pets, and I never had any, not until we came to Bigby Farm."

In that short exchange, the little girl offered more information about herself than he'd ever known. Her dislike of the animals and chores was more about wanting to please her brother than it was about her own desires.

"We have a farm, but it's nowhere near as big as Bigby Farm," Elena said. "Don't you just love living on a farm?"

The gleam in Faith's eyes gave him hope. "I've always wanted to live on a farm," she whispered." Then she let out a long sigh. "But my brother says I'm stupid because of it."

Elena made a face. "He doesn't sound very nice."

A strange expression crossed Faith's face. Then she nodded. "You're right. He isn't very nice. He's been mean to me a lot lately, and I've been letting him, because I've been sad that my dad left us, and I was sad, too."

Elena looked at her sympathetically. "Your dad left you?"

As Faith nodded, Elena touched the little girl's arm. "It's okay if you're sad. My mom died, and even though I was little, I was sad about not having a mom."

Then she looked up at Charlotte and smiled. "But I have a new mom now, and it's more wonderful than I ever imagined it would be."

Charlotte gave Elena an affectionate squeeze. "I'm so glad to hear you say that. Being your mother has been the greatest honor anyone has ever given me."

Elena smiled back at her, then turned to Faith. "Maybe, like me getting a new mother, you'll get a new dad. And you could even get a baby sister, just like me."

He could feel Enid's eyes on him. Everyone knew she was hoping for another successful match. But he didn't think the older woman appreciated the difficulty of making that happen with so many things going on around them. He couldn't ask Madison to get involved in a relationship when she was dealing with so many other things. And, the kids needed to be in a more stable place before he even thought about bringing that complication into their lives.

Though he liked Madison well enough and he enjoyed spending time with her, and he definitely was attracted to her, a romance was a different level of relationship, and he wasn't sure how that would play out. Maybe it would be just fine, but there was a big difference in liking someone enough to be interested in them and marrying them. He and Madison were nowhere close to being there.

Especially since he hadn't told her about his money. Sharing that part of himself was hard after spending so many years wondering if people liked him or his money. Now that he was comfortable, knowing people liked him, how would they feel about him, knowing he had money?

"My first dad wasn't that great," Faith said quietly. "I'm not sure I want another one."

"Well, if you need one for the daddy daughter dance at school, you can borrow mine," Elena said.

It was a touching gesture, and even Faith seemed to appreciate it. She nodded slowly. "And if you ever want to come out to Bigby Farm to see our animals, I'd be happy to give you a tour."

Elena turned and looked at Charlotte. "Can I? Please?"

Charlotte nodded. "I'm sure we can make arrangements."

Then Charlotte looked apologetically at Wade. "I hate to leave when it seems like the girls are getting along so well, but we have someplace to be. I need to buy some of Allie's salve. She's given me the recipe dozens of times to make it for myself, but mine never turns out as good."

When Charlotte left, Faith turned to Enid. "Is it okay if I invite Elena over soon? I miss my old friends, and I'd like to have someone other than my brother to talk to."

Enid grinned. "Friends are like treasures, and we're always happy to have them."

Then Faith turned to Wade. "It was nice of Elena to say her dad could also be there for me, but if there's a dance at school, and I need a father, will you come instead? Even when my dad was around, he promised to come, but never did. He was always stuck in meetings."

Then she looked up at him and frowned. "How come you're not married and have kids? You're pretty old."

A lot of reasons, but none that would make sense to a little girl. "I guess I just haven't found the right person," he said.

"I suppose you could marry my mom, but she might not want to get married again. But maybe it won't be so bad, since you're a lot nicer than my dad."

Enid snickered, and before Wade could respond, D.J. plowed into his sister. "How dare you say that? You traitor."

The little boy started pounding his sister, and Wade quickly jumped in to pull him off. "Don't touch me," D.J. screamed.

Josh ran in to grab the flailing boy. "Hey, buddy. Easy now. There's no reason for violence."

D.J. punched Josh in the stomach. "Yes, there is! She's given up on our dad coming back. Well, I won't. Never!" Then he turned and glared at Wade. "And I'll never let you marry my mom. You can be as nice to me as you want, but it's not going to work. I'm not going to learn your stupid programming on your stupid computer. It probably hasn't been updated since before I was born."

Wherever the boy's father was, Wade hoped he was proud of himself for the little monster he'd created. Though he knew Hayden was already looking into Dave from a legal standpoint, maybe it wouldn't hurt to do some digging of his own.

"Have it your way," Wade said. "I was just trying to help."

Faith came to stand beside him. "I'd like to learn about computers. If we stayed in my old school, I would have gotten to take a computer programming class."

"Traitor," D.J. said, making a fist.

"There will be no more hitting your sister," Wade said firmly. "I'm sure your dad wouldn't like hearing you've been hurting her."

"He wouldn't like hearing that she gave up on him, either."

It wasn't as though the man had gone missing. He'd run away. But as many times as they'd tried telling D.J., the boy seemed to ignore it. It was obviously too painful for the child to admit.

And who would admit to their father not wanting them? Maybe that was the problem. They were trying so hard to get D.J. to accept the truth, and it was just forcing him deeper into denial. Maybe it was time to try another tactic.

"You're right," Wade said. "I'm sure your dad would be real proud of you for defending him the way you do. You're just trying to help your family in his absence. I get that. It's a lot of responsibility, isn't it?"

D.J. stared at him suspiciously. "What kind of trick are you trying to pull now?"

"None. It just occurred to me that it has to be hard, listening to people say bad things about your dad all the time. I'm sorry. I'm sure there's a reasonable explanation for him to be staying away so long."

"Exactly. He has important work to do and can't tell us about it. Maybe he's even with the CIA or something."

Lord, please help this little boy.

"I'm sure he'd want to know that you were taking care of things, listening to your mom, taking care of your sisters. I don't know the guy, but I don't think he'd appreciate you hitting your sister."

D.J. looked thoughtful, then frowned. "He didn't like it when Faith and I fought over stuff."

"Is that what you want him to hear about the next time you see him?" Wade asked.

Faith came and slipped her hand in D.J.'s. "I'm sorry for what I said about Mom getting married again. I just think she's probably lonely without Dad. Look at how hard she's working. She's eating healthy and even though she doesn't go to a gym, the work we do is kind of like working out. She's trying to get skinny again."

Did the kids really think Madison would take that scumbag back? And what about the breakthrough he'd thought Faith had, realizing that maybe their dad wasn't so perfect, after all?

But her words seemed to calm D.J. down. "Yeah, she is. I didn't think about that. She has lost some weight. Maybe she just doesn't want us to get our hopes up."

"You know how she is."

It felt wrong to let this conversation continue, but Enid put her hand on his back. "Let it be," she said quietly.

If Enid, who wasn't known for her gentle approach to things, would say that, then he'd do as she asked. Still, it felt odd to let the children spin their fantasies that their father would come back and everything would magically be okay. Maybe this was confirmation that Wade needed to do what he could to find their father. Who knew? Maybe the guy would man up and take care of his children.

CHAPTER 8

"*A* watched pot never boils," Allie said, giving Madison a playful shove as she carried another box of hand-made lavender soap into the store room. "I'm sure the kids are fine with Wade."

Madison had been working all day, setting the gift shop to rights, when she went into the store room to get a few more items for display. Some of Allie's products had been featured on a morning news show in Twin Falls, and suddenly, people were coming from all over the state to purchase some of Allie's lavender products.

"Here, let me help you." Madison grabbed some of the items out of Allie's arms, and helped her set them with the rest of the soaps.

"Thank you. You're a lifesaver."

"Don't mention it. It looks like you're finally catching up on all the orders."

Allie nodded. "Yes. I'm sorry I haven't been in here to help you as much lately, but creation is what I do, and the business stuff is beyond me."

Madison laughed as her cousin threw up her arms. It was

true that Allie didn't have much business sense, but she always thought that the other woman gave herself far less credit than she deserved.

"Maybe, but you've really grown your business. Just a few months ago, you'd lost everything in the Christmas fire. But with your new barn, and the publicity from the barn raising, it seems like your business is better than ever."

Allie grabbed a box from under the table. "Yes, and that's exactly what I want to talk you about. The business end is making me crazy, and you've done a fantastic job of running the shop with my attention being so diverted."

Allie gestured around the inside of the gift shop. "Even though my employees do a nice job of keeping things looking straightened, you've added touches that make it extra special. My inventory has never been more accurate or up-to-date, and all details are always perfectly taken care of. No more calls from vendors because I forgot to put a bill in the mail."

High praise, and yet Madison didn't see it as being anything special. "It's what I've done all these years running a household. You keep your records in order, and you make sure the bills are paid on time."

Madison shrugged as she pulled out the tablet and added, "I had to get even better at it once Dave left. I learned very quickly how to maximize what I had and to keep track of everything."

"But that's exactly what I mean." Allie yanked the tablet out of her hands. "All this? This is Greek to me. I barely even know how to work this device, let alone input all the information the way you're doing. And then, to do it right now, without being on a time crunch because of some weird tax deadline…"

Madison couldn't help laughing. "Tax deadlines aren't weird. They're consistent for planning purposes."

"Like I ever know what day it is."

"You have a point. But that's why you have so many people helping you," Madison said, smiling. "Now give me back the tablet so I can finish entering the new soap in the inventory."

"First, I want to talk to you about something and I want your full attention."

The grin on Allie's face made it impossible for Madison to think she was in trouble. But what could Allie possibly have to talk about that was so important?

"You have it. What's up?"

"I was talking to Hayden and Andrew about my business organization, and they think I'm still trying to do too much with running the day to day operation. I've already hired Wade as my farm manager, but they think I should hire someone else to manage my retail business."

"Is Wade doing a bad job?" Madison asked.

Allie shook her head. "Not at all. He's amazing. But we're spreading him too thin, and with the extra attention my products are getting, he can't do it all. So we're dividing up the job into farm operations and retail operations. Since Wade is better with the farm stuff, I need someone on the retail end. I want you to be my retail manager. Andrew says he's never seen my books look so good, and Hayden was threatening to steal you from me for Caroline's projects. So I'll just tell you right now, whatever Hayden offers you, I'll double."

"You can't afford it," Hayden said, entering the shop. "But if Madison really wants to work with you instead of helping Caroline and me, either by helping manage the day camp or taking over the reservations for the guest stays, I'll let you have her."

Madison stared at him. "Are you two really fighting over me?"

Hayden shrugged. "I've had a lot of PA's in my time, and you're better than all of them."

"Which means I need her more," Allie said. "You at least know what you need, whereas I'm floundering without Madison."

The desperation on Allie's face was adorable. But as Madison looked from Allie to Hayden, she realized they were serious.

"I don't understand," Madison said. "I'm just doing what anyone would do."

Both Hayden and Allie turned to stare at her.

"No, you're not. That's the point. You're doing an amazing job, and you need to be recognized for it," Allie said. "I'd love for you to keep working with me as my retail manager, but if you really want to work with Caroline and Hayden, you can."

From people refusing to interview her because she had no work experience, to two people fighting over who got to work with her…it was almost unbelievable. All those years of Dave telling her she wasn't smart or couldn't do it, and that her talents lie with the children, weighed on her. Even though she'd spent a lot of time since her divorce telling herself that so many of Dave's words were lies, she hadn't realized just how deep they'd gone. He was the only one who mocked her for her weight. And he was the only one who'd ever put her down for not being smart.

The previous week's sermon had been about who God said you were. And even though it hadn't specifically said so, there was nothing about God's definition of you depending on your size, your skills, your intelligence, or any of the other things the world put value on. Tears filled her eyes as she realized that she'd been believing so many lies about herself for so long.

She'd thought her newfound cousins were doing everything for her because they loved her, because of grace. But there was so much more to their actions than that. They loved her, *and* they thought she was smart and capable.

"Are you okay?" Allie asked, setting the tablet on the table, then putting her arms around Madison. "I didn't mean to put pressure on you. Don't feel obligated because we're family. I'm sure you could get a dozen better jobs, I just thought—"

"No." Madison tried brushing at her eyes, but her arm was pinned to her side from Allie's hug. "You don't understand. It's been a long time since anyone has believed in me. And until now, I hadn't realized just how much I needed it."

Allie gave her another squeeze. "That's what family is for. We believe in you."

Then Allie turned to look over at Hayden. "If it weren't for Andrew, Gram, Caroline, and Hayden, I wouldn't have believed in me either. But they taught me that I can follow my dreams, and because of their faith in me, that's exactly what I'm doing."

She remembered the emails they'd exchanged as Allie was beginning her lavender business, taking it from a hobby to a full-time enterprise. She'd been in awe of Allie and her passion.

"But what if I don't have a dream like your lavender business? My only dream has ever been for my family. Before Dave left, I just wanted to make everything okay between us. And now, I just want to be able to provide a good life for my kids, and for them to heal from the divorce and be happy again."

Sighing, she looked around the room. "Don't get me wrong. I enjoy this work, and I like that I'm helping. But it doesn't consume me the way your lavender consumes you."

"Who said it has to?" Hayden asked. "For me, it's all about

supporting Caroline and her passion. I spent a lot of years doing a job I hated for all the wrong reasons. Running a farm day camp and turning this place into a vacation destination, it's not about those things for me. I just want to keep Bigby Farm in the hands of the people who love it. But mostly, it's about the light in my wife's eyes when she's teaching kids about the animals, or showing some city folk how to adapt some of the clean living ideas from Bigby Farm for their own homes. Your passion is supporting your children and their dreams. And that's perfectly fine."

Madison couldn't help giving him a hug. Though the connection with Hayden was the briefest of hugs, Madison knew she'd found one more piece of a forever family she didn't realize was missing from her life. It was one thing to have the comfort of other women telling you that you were valuable, but Dave and his friends had constantly put her down as just a housewife.

"Hey, can I get in on this hug-fest?" Wade asked from the shop doorway. "I sure could use one right about now."

She stepped out of Hayden's embrace and smiled at him. "Of course. Were the children that bad? Where are they?"

Wade pointed over his shoulder. "Helping Enid bring in her finds from the farmers' market. She's got her friend Mona with her. Mona wants to take Enid zip lining, and they've promised to bring the kids if they help with a few things first."

She wasn't sure which part was more shocking—old ladies zip lining, or that the kids were being cooperative.

"But Gram's like, a hundred years old. And Mona has to be even older. Surely they won't do something so dangerous. This isn't some weird stunt to get the kids to help, is it?" Madison asked.

Hayden coughed. "Don't ever say that in front of them."

"True." Allie laughed. "They're both in their eighties, which you should know by now. Don't you dare accuse them of being older to their faces."

Okay, fine. She did know that. "But she's so old, and fragile. What if they break her?"

Everyone except Madison laughed.

Wade walked over to her and put his arm around her. "It's nice to know you care. But trust me, nothing keeps Enid down for long. Have you ever seen Mona's motorcycle?"

Madison turned to stare at him. "She has a motorcycle?"

"She's kind of a thrill junkie, and she has a club with Enid and her friends called The Grannies. They basically do all the dangerous stuff they can think of to make sure everyone else in the community has the same amount of gray hair as they do," Wade said.

"Oh stop," Allie said. "They aren't that bad. I love the idea that they want to live life to the fullest while they still have life to live. We could all learn from that."

Hayden shook his head. "Just run for cover if you see Mona on her motorcycle."

Allie shook her head. "They're harmless. And they go zip lining every couple of weeks. It's perfectly safe. Now, Mona's dream of bungee jumping off the Perrine bridge in Twin Falls..." She let out an exasperated sigh. "We've managed to discourage her so far."

Madison took a step toward the door. "Maybe I should go make sure Mona doesn't put any ideas into the kids' heads."

"They're fine." Wade blocked her from going farther. "On the ride home, Faith was grilling Mona about the safety of zip lining and if they could wear helmets. She asked more questions than any mother I know."

Madison couldn't help smiling. Her daughter could be quite the mother hen when she wanted to. "I take it all this means things went well at the farmers' market?"

"In a manner of speaking." Wade looked over at the shop entrance, then back at her. "It was rocky at first, and D.J. ran off. But we found him, and I had a talk with him. He feels betrayed that no one is waiting around for his father to come home. He still thinks that one day, his dad will walk through the door, and everything will magically be okay."

Madison let out a long sigh. "Did you get him to see reason?"

"No. That hasn't been working, so I tried something else. I asked him what he thought his dad would think if he came home to find out how his son was behaving. I challenged him to be better so his dad would be proud of him when he came home."

Did he realize the unrealistic expectations he'd set up? "He's not coming home. He's at some ashram in India finding himself. There's no phone, no internet, nothing. Trust me, I've tried everything."

Hayden nodded. "It's like the guy dropped off the face of the earth. I've gone through all the legal channels to find him, but he doesn't want to be found. A man who's coming back for his kids doesn't make it so hard."

Then Hayden made a disgusted noise. "Of course, if I owed as much money as he does, I probably wouldn't come back either. He invested in so many scams and had so many secret accounts, it should be illegal. As far as I can tell, there was nothing illegal in his actions, but he definitely skirted the line."

Hayden's analysis was still hard to take, even though her lawyer had basically told her the same thing. Worse, though, was seeing the looks of pity on Wade's and Allie's faces.

"That's part of why I'm so diligent with your books," Madison said, looking over at Allie. "I'd ask Dave about discrepancies in some of the account information, and he'd tell me I was remembering wrong. For a long time, I believed him. And when I was faced with the final accounting, I wished I'd pushed harder. I was just so afraid of making our marriage worse if I made waves, and I was so used to being told I was stupid, I figured it was just me."

Madison straightened. "But now I know better, and I keep track of everything, because I don't want it biting me later."

"You're not stupid," Wade said, sounding disgusted.

"No, I'm not. But I believed it for a long time."

The children must have finished whatever task Gram had given them, because they came running into the gift shop.

"Mom! Gram's friend Mona wants to take us zip lining. She says going with kids makes her feel young again. Can we go?"

The enthusiasm in D.J.'s voice was too hard to refuse. Not when he'd been so sullen for so long. She didn't like that Wade had given her son false hope, but she had to say, the change was remarkable.

"What did Gram say? Did you do all the work she asked you to do?"

Faith nodded. "I even helped her chop up some more rutabagas. She said she's going to try fermenting them. Whatever that is."

"Oh no. Not this nightmare again." Allie pushed past them. "I've got to do an intervention. Trust me when I say the rutabaga fermentation experiment is not going to end well. She tried it before and nearly killed us all with food poisoning. If she tries to get you to eat a fermented rutabaga, just say no."

The kids looked at Allie like they weren't planning on it, but Allie was already out the door.

Madison turned her attention back to the kids. "If it's okay with Gram, fine by me. But I think I should go with you to supervise. I understand Mona can be a little…interesting at times."

D.J. let out a whoop, and as she looked over at their eager faces, they looked happier than they had in a long time. She just hoped it would last when they realized their father was never coming back.

CHAPTER 9

*A*s far as Wade was concerned, Dave McKay was the lowest form of pond scum on the planet. He didn't deserve the hero-worship in his son's eyes. But the kids weren't going to be able to move on without some kind of closure with the jerk.

"I don't think those papers in your hand deserve to be mangled so badly," Allie said, entering the office. "What's going on?"

"Sorry. I was just thinking."

"About killing paper? Or someone else?" Allie grinned, then took the papers out of his hand. "This looks like information about Madison's ex. Does Madison know you have them?"

He snatched the papers back. "I got them from Hayden. He might have run out of contacts, but I haven't."

"Yes, but if Dave clearly doesn't want to be found, then maybe we should leave well enough alone." Her expression turned serious. "Meddling in other people's lives never ends well, even when your heart is in the right place."

"Someone's got to do something," he said. "Those kids are hurting, and they need answers."

"And what if those answers hurt more than they help? Maybe you need to take a step back and think about what your real motivation is here."

He stared at her for a minute. "And what do you mean by that?"

"I know you like Madison. I don't blame you. She's amazing. And I can see where it would be difficult to get involved now, given all the things going on. But maybe you're trying to rush things, wanting to fix the situation faster. Maybe, what you really need is time. The kids will eventually figure out what a jerk their father is. They're not stupid. But if Madison is the woman for you, she'll still be around when the time is right."

Her words stung, and she made it sound like he was being selfish. But he wasn't the selfish one.

"I get what you're saying, but I don't think you're giving me enough credit. I know there isn't an easy fix, but it doesn't seem right to me that this guy completely gets away with what he's done without any consequences."

Allie gave him a harsh look. "And who are you? God? That seems like an even worse motivation." Then her expression softened. "Leave it alone. Everything will work itself out in due time. You've got to trust that God has a plan, even if you don't understand it yet."

"I'm not trying to play God. I just want to help a little boy who's lost." He hadn't even thought of it in terms of a relationship with Madison. But the way Allie looked at him, she acted like it was his only motivation.

"We haven't even gotten D.J. in to see the psychologist yet," Allie said. "At least wait until after that consultation to see if tracking down Dave is going to be the best thing for him."

He let out a long sigh as he nodded. "I suppose, in the grand scheme of things, a few weeks isn't a long time. I just..."

Feel frustrated that a man could get away with hurting people the way Dave has.

"All right, I'll back off. I was just trying to help."

As Allie nodded, he thought about what she'd said. Though he hadn't made his feelings for Madison a secret, he also hadn't been broadcasting it. "Wait a second. Who says I like Madison?"

Allie grinned. "We're not stupid. You've spent too many years keeping yourself isolated from anyone you might possibly care about. You'd only take as much interest in Madison as you are if you really liked her."

Allie gave him an encouraging smile. "And for the record, I approve completely. I've always thought that you were a great catch. You have a lot to offer a woman, and I wish more men were as warmhearted and compassionate as you. You hide it underneath that gruff exterior, but you have a heart of gold."

He didn't know what to say. The only time he'd been described as a catch was back in his Silicon Valley days, when people based such decisions on the size of a man's bank account. Not even Allie knew his net worth, so he knew her praise had nothing to do with that. Even though he believed a person ought to be judged by their character, he hadn't had much experience of that being how women saw him. One more thing he didn't feel comfortable sharing with Allie. He liked her as a friend, but not as someone he felt safe opening up to.

And yet, he immediately thought about Madison. Even though they'd never talked much about their personal lives with one another, something inside him knew that it would be very easy to talk to her about it. He still thought about their conversation at the ice cream shop. It had been a long time since he'd had such a deep conversation with someone. He just felt a connection to Madison unlike anything he'd felt before. Even that didn't seem safe to share with Allie, who'd see it as a sign they belonged together.

Wade left the office, intent on getting some work done. But all he could think about was Madison. Even though he'd already admitted to himself that he liked her, it was weird coming to terms with the idea of just how much. Allie had brought up a good point, that he mostly avoided people. Preferring his own company. But he did tend to seek Madison out. There was something about being around her that comforted him.

Just then, he spied Madison walking back from the mailbox, obviously upset.

As he approached, he called out, "Madison. What's wrong?"

Tears rolled down her face as she held up a piece of paper. "I'm being sued. By Dave's old business partner. The last time I talked to him, he was nice about the fact that I had been left just as destitute as everyone else. But he was visiting an old friend in Twin Falls and saw a news program about Allie's lavender business. Since he saw me in the background, he seems to think that I was being less than honest about my financial situation. So he's decided to sue me anyway."

Wade took the papers out of her hand and scanned them. "This says you were an officer of the company. That's not true, is it?"

Madison nodded. "Actually, I am. Dave thought it would be a good idea to have a family business, and so he made me an officer. Honestly, I didn't know anything about his business. It was a mistake, I know. I can't tell you how many times Dave would hand me a stack of papers and tell me to sign off on them and I would just do it. Married people are supposed to be on each other's accounts, aren't they? A couple of times, I would look at them, but when I asked questions, he told me I wouldn't understand. He used to like telling me I was stupid, and I believed him for a long time. I know that isn't true now, but I am more than paying for that mistake."

It happened a lot more often than people thought, wives being part of a husband's corporation but not really knowing the business. But David's business partner should have known that.

Wade frowned. "This lawsuit is just a desperate attempt to get money where there is none."

"Desperate or not, I'm being sued. I know he thinks I can afford it, but we all know that's a joke. I know that Hayden will be happy to help, but it bothers me that I have to deal with it."

Even though he'd told Allie he was going to stay out of it, he couldn't just let this go. It was wrong that Madison had to keep looking over her shoulder, waiting for the next person to go after her. At some point, Dave had to answer for his actions. And even though Hayden should be able to file all the necessary paperwork to make this one disappear, what happened when the next one came around?

This had to stop.

"It's not fair," Wade said.

Madison gave him a smile. "It's not fair, but it's reality. At least I'm not doing it alone. It means a lot to me to have your support and friendship."

She paused for a moment, then looked at him. "I know I shouldn't say this, but you give me strength I didn't know I had. Thanks to you, I feel like I can stand up for myself more, because of how you stand up for me. I just wanted you to know."

Even though Allie had warned him against rushing things, he had to respond. "I understand. I feel the same way.

I was just in talking with Allie, and she made me think of a lot of things I wanted to say, but I thought about how I would have been more comfortable talking to you about it."

She smiled at him. "I feel the same way about you. Maybe, when our lives settle down, we can talk it all out."

Okay, fine. Message received. Everyone wanted him to wait on starting something with Madison. He could do that. But that didn't mean Madison had to keep suffering for her ex's stupidity. He'd let Hayden tackle the legal portion, but it was time to take action on the rest. According to Hayden, Dave hadn't broken any laws or been charged with any crimes, other than the contempt of court charges.

Based on what Wade knew of the financial situation, and his quick glance at the lawsuit, it looked like Dave was taking out loans, then borrowing money to repay them. Then he'd borrow more money to repay that loan. But where did the original money go? Where did the money he was making go? According to the paperwork, Madison had over a hundred thousand dollars in debt, thanks to Dave.

Where were all these so-called investments? He tried remembering the names from the financial documents he'd seen. And then it hit him. A solution that might solve all of their problems. He just needed to talk to Liam.

CHAPTER 10

The past few weeks had felt to Madison like the family was entering a new normal. Hayden had gotten the lawsuit dismissed, and it seemed some of the weight had been lifted off her shoulders.

"Mom! Guess what?" The wide grin on D.J.'s face never failed to make her heart happy.

It had been a long time since she'd seen her son smile like that. And lately, those smiles were becoming more and more common.

"What?"

She closed the computer screen and walked around her desk to greet him.

"You know that computer program I'm working on to learn how to make my own game?"

Madison nodded. Having Wade around had been a very good for her family. D.J. was creating his own computer game. Rather than being obsessed with making everyone miserable, he was now obsessed with creating this game, and being a good brother and son so that his dad would be proud of him.

"That's wonderful," she said. "I'm so impressed with the progress you've made."

D.J.'s face lit up. "Do you think Dad will like it? I sent another email to his old email address, telling him about my progress. Dr. Hart says it's good for me to express my feelings that way, but I shouldn't expect an answer."

Madison nodded slowly. Dr. Hart had been recommended to them by Andrew's colleague and was helping D.J. sort through his anger over his father's abandonment. While he didn't think it was harmful for D.J. to live his life as if his father were coming back, he was also helping the family figure out ways for the boy to cope when he came to the inevitable conclusion that his father would never return.

"That's great. I'm so happy to hear it. Can you do me a favor and take those boxes into the store?"

She pointed to some boxes of lavender skincare products that Allie had just made. Now that they were in inventory, Madison wanted them out in the gift shop as quickly as possible.

D.J. smiled. "Sure. Does this count as my time helping you? Wade says that for every hour I help you, he'll spend an hour working with me on my game."

Madison smiled. "Of course it does."

He picked up the boxes, and she gathered the rest, and they went into the main shop area. Madison turned to go back to her office, but was stopped in her tracks as a man entered the gift shop.

"Hey everyone," Wade said.

Wade?

He had shaved, cut his hair, and was dressed in a nice suit. She didn't know he even owned a suit.

Wade grinned. "I clean up pretty good, don't I? I never thought I would end up in this monkey suit again, but I have to fly out to California to meet with some people. My friend

Liam is putting together a new project, and he asked for my help. I'll only be gone a few days, and everything here seems to be going smoothly."

Madison tried to form words in response, but her mouth wouldn't work. She'd never thought Wade bad looking, but without all the scruff and dressed like a businessman, he was the kind of guy her younger self would have drooled over. And okay, fine. She might be drooling just a little now.

D.J. walked over to him. "Wow, I didn't know you knew how to shave. You should wear a suit more often. People would respect you more."

Wade smiled as he patted her son gently on the shoulder. "You might be right, but I would be careful of people who judge you only by your outward appearance. Just because someone looks good on the outside doesn't mean they're good on the inside. I want people to judge me for my inside, but as Allie has pointed out many times, my outside was starting to get a little scary."

Madison laughed. She'd heard both Allie and Caroline tease Wade about scaring off the children who were here for the summer day camps. But oddly enough, most of the children flocked to him.

"I'm going over to Mona's," Gram said, entering the shop. "She's got a belly dancing instructor coming over, and since Layla says I need more exercise, I'm going to join them. Layla is with the girls in the garden."

Then Gram turned her attention to Wade. "It's about time you cleaned up that ugly mug of yours. Such a handsome man, hiding behind all that disgusting hair. I never did like my men hairy. Why, when Edward was alive, he shaved twice a day so that his cheeks were always smooth as a baby's butt. Makes for good smooching."

A wicked grin filled Gram's face, and Madison couldn't help smiling.

Wade ran his hand over his cheek. "It does feel strange, not having anything here. But I'd forgotten what a pain shaving was. Besides, my beard was actually quite soft. Allie had made me some beard oil, and it's really popular here in the shop."

He pointed at one of the displays.

Gram made a noise. "People these days are foolish in how they spend their money on such ridiculous notions. I don't know why they don't just make it for themselves, the way Allie does. You know, I taught her all this stuff. It's a shame that people don't spend more time with their elders, learning from them. My children have never wanted to have anything to do with me, calling my ways crazy. But at least you all see sense."

Then Gram looked around the shop and grinned. "But I thank God that there are some stupid people left in the world, too helpless to do things for themselves. Our Allie is making quite the name for herself because of it, and I have to say that it is nice having money for some extras."

Wade chuckled. "Only you would thank God for stupid people."

Gram brought her attention back to Wade. "Now that you don't look like a hooligan, are you going to ask Madison out? You two need to hurry up and get married. None of my other grandchildren seem to be very interested in making great-grandchildren for me, and since Madison obviously knows how to make babies, maybe the two of you can give me some more."

Madison looked over at D.J. to gauge his reaction. His face was expressionless, so hopefully it meant he was finally starting to lose his attachment to the idea that someday his father would return, and they would get back together.

Gram nudged Wade. "That wasn't a suggestion. I don't know why you're so stubborn. You're not going to do any better than my granddaughter, and I know you two like each other, so you might as well ask her out."

Wade shook his head. "That's a private matter between me and Madison. She needs time to heal from her divorce, and I want to give her the space she needs."

Gram stomped her foot. "Do you like her or not?"

Wade let out a long sigh. "Of course I like her. What's not to like? But I also respect her, and she's made it clear that she's not ready for anything other than friendship. I know you think you can push everyone around and get your own way, and most of the time, that works. But when it comes to people's hearts, you need to let them take their time and do what's best for them."

It meant a lot to hear that Wade was working so hard to be considerate of her feelings. And not just her feelings, but her children's. She stole a glance at D.J., who looked thoughtful, but still not upset.

"I'm not getting any younger," Gram said. "You people act like you have all the time in the world, but let me tell you, life is shorter than you think, and if you care about someone, then you need to say it, and act on it, because you might not have tomorrow."

Though she had a point, Madison couldn't help thinking that it wasn't as simple as all that. Yes, she liked Wade. And it was more than a friend kind of like. Nor could she deny that she found him attractive. She'd thought so even before his transformation. But she'd made this mistake before. Her relationship with Dave had started out because he'd been the best-looking guy who'd ever paid her any bit of attention, and he'd often told her that she was the cutest girl he'd ever seen.

But then she stopped being cute, and she'd learned that there was more to a marriage than finding the other person attractive, and that breathless desire that had driven them in the early years of their relationship. They'd been talking a lot about the difference between love and lust in church, and that discussion had carried over into the adult small divorce recovery group she'd been attending. She wouldn't make that same mistake again.

Wade smiled at Madison, then turned his attention to Enid. "I understand what you're saying, and I agree that life is short. But I'm not going to make a decision about forever based on this feeling of pressure."

He squared his shoulders. "I love you like family, Enid. But you have to back off. You need to accept that I'm giving Madison space precisely because I do care about her. And I would think that, because you care about her, you would want the same for her."

He looked at Madison and smiled. "I know you think you're fat, and maybe you do have a few extra curves. But that's one of the things I find attractive about you. But that isn't the only reason I like you. You're smart, funny, kind, and you treat people with respect, even if you think they're a homeless guy. You're the only person outside of the Bigbys who's ever tried to get to know me on a deeper level. It's probably the Bigby in you, but it's also because you're a good woman."

Madison didn't know what to say. Tears tickled the backs of her eyes, but this wasn't the time or place for her to express those emotions. He'd just said all the words she'd needed to hear from her ex-husband and hadn't.

And here was Wade, proving that he saw her as a person, but more importantly, he saw her heart.

If he asked her out today, she would say yes. And if he kissed her, she would kiss him back, and that might lead to other things. Or maybe not, because Wade respected her, and he didn't see her as just a conquest.

Enid made a noise. "It sounds like you're already in love

with her. And I'm pretty sure she's in love with you, too. But go on ahead and be stubborn about it, because that's what all my foolish grandchildren have done. I think everyone's holding out on giving me more great-grandchildren on principle."

Allie had just come in from the back, but she stopped and started to slink away.

"I saw you," Gram said. "Don't think you can get away so easily."

Before Allie could respond, Caroline pushed past her and entered the room. "Just stop. We all know you mean well, and we love you for it. But you also don't know how much your words hurt sometimes. I respect Wade and Madison for taking things slowly and doing what they think is best for their relationship."

Caroline gestured at D.J. "Have you thought about how he feels, considering he's still mourning the loss of his father? You complain that he hasn't warmed to you the way the others have. But maybe, if you looked at what's important to him, you would see that he isn't ready to have a new father forced on him. And you should be grateful that Wade and Madison are giving him the time and therapy he needs to get over the loss of his father before thrusting one more change in his life."

Then Caroline squared her shoulders. "As for your baby comments, stop. Just stop. You have no idea the pressure you're putting on all of us, especially me. I wanted to keep this private, because I don't want everyone hovering, but I lost a baby a couple months ago. I wasn't very far along, but it still hurts. I hate hearing all this talk about babies, when all I want to do is lay in bed and cry because I don't understand why I had to lose mine."

She turned to leave, and ran into Allie, who put her arms around her, and guided her into the back room.

Madison had been watching Gram during Caroline's confession, and she saw the older woman's face crumble.

"I didn't know," Gram said. "What have I done? I never wanted to hurt anyone. I thought I was helping."

Her eyes filled with tears as she looked up at Madison. "Is that how you feel about me, pushing you and Wade together?"

Madison went to her grandmother and put her arms around her. "I know you're doing it out of love, and I wouldn't say it hurts the way it does Caroline, but yes, it's a lot of pressure. I'm trying to do the right thing, and to make better decisions about my life than I did before. Because yes, I like Wade. I think he is all the things that he thinks about me, but I don't know if I'm ready for a relationship yet. I want to do better this time around. So please give me and everyone else the space we need to make good decisions for our lives."

She gave her grandmother a gentle squeeze. "You have no idea how much we love and appreciate all the support you've given us. We all know how much you love us, and sometimes we don't speak up because we don't want to hurt your feelings. But look around at the wonderful family we have. Appreciate what you've got now, and even though it would be nice for you and for all of us to get to have more babies to hold, if this is all God has planned for our family, isn't it still the most wonderful thing ever?"

Gram squeezed her so tight, she could barely breathe. She could feel Gram's tears wetting her shirt as the old woman sobbed.

"I never meant to push any of you away. My children all say that I was too controlling and pushy. I don't want to make that same mistake with you all as I did with them. You've obviously learned from your mistakes or are at least trying to. I hope I can learn from mine."

Madison pressed a kiss on top of her grandmother's head. "I believe you already are. And while I know you're working things out with your children, maybe it's time you told them the things that you just told me. Deep down, I think they still love you and they still want a relationship with you, but when there are so many years of hurt between you, it's hard to know how to take that first step forward."

Gram pulled away. "Thank you. You're right."

Then she glanced in the direction of the closed door to the store room. "I need to go apologize to Caroline. I didn't realize she'd lost a baby, and having done so myself, I know how much it hurts. I had no idea my words were hurting her more."

Madison let Gram go, and she brushed at the tears in her eyes. "Well, that was unexpected. Nothing like a little drama to liven things up on Bigby Farm."

Wade shifted nervously. "It seems like there's a lot that needs to be said here. A lot of the things, I wish I could have said to you privately."

Madison nodded. She also would have preferred that this conversation had taken place privately, especially given that her son was still staring at them, an expression she didn't recognize on his face. But hopefully, he, too, had gotten something out of the discussion.

She turned her attention back to Wade and smiled. "Definitely. At least some good has been done here. Maybe we can continue this conversation when you get back."

"I'd like that," Wade said giving a smile that melted her clear down to her toes. "Maybe we could go for coffee or something."

It was cute, the way he stumbled over his words, like a nervous teenager trying to ask her on a date but wasn't sure if he could call it a date or not. She wasn't sure if they could call it a date.

But she smiled at him. "I'd like that a lot," she said. "Let's make it a priority."

Wade grinned as he left the shop, leaving a giddy feeling in the pit of Madison's stomach. She reminded herself that the giddy feeling wasn't what it was about. But she couldn't help feeling excited anyway.

She held out her hand to her son. "That was a lot to listen to, wasn't it? How about we get some ice cream from Gram's fridge and talk about it?"

After the lavender ice cream incident, Gram had taken to going by Lik's on a regular basis to see what other new flavors they had come up with. Because Lik's was committed to local and healthy options, they always had a couple of flavors suitable for diabetics. Though Graham still had to eat it in moderation, it was nice to have some treats around the house.

D.J. nodded. "Just you and me?"

Madison gave him a smile. "Just you and me. I want to hear more about your video game."

Even though she was eager to gauge her son's reaction to the conversation he'd just witnessed, she didn't want to put too much pressure on him, especially since she didn't want to risk hurting any of the progress he'd made.

As they walked to the house to get ice cream, D.J. looked up at her. "Are you lonely without Dad?"

She'd been lonely with him, but she hadn't realized just how much until coming to Bigby Farm. And that wasn't something her son would understand—being married to someone who made you feel so miserable and lonely but accepting it because you thought that's what you were supposed to do.

Instead, she smiled at him and said, "Yes. It's a different kind of lonely, wanting to have that special someone to share your life with. But it's like I said in there. It's important to me to do the right thing, and I don't want to be with someone just because I'm lonely. I want to be in a relationship because it's what's right for me, and what's right for you guys."

D.J. nodded slowly. "You like Wade though, don't you?"

Madison nodded. "I do. He's a good man. And I like how he treats people. I like that he's someone we can all count on."

Then she looked out at his truck driving off in the distance. "But I also like how he treats me."

D.J. stopped, then turned and looked at her. "Dad wasn't very nice to you."

It was the first admission that his father had been less-than-perfect, and while part of her wanted to cheer, she knew she had to tread carefully. "No, he wasn't."

"He used to call you fat and stupid. Sometimes I heard him call you other bad names. Wade has never said anything bad about you."

She shook her head and held out her hand. "No, he hasn't. We could learn a lot about how to treat other people from Wade."

D.J. took her hand, and she gave it a squeeze. The past few months, he'd been so focused on trying to be a man and proving himself that her little boy had gotten lost in there somewhere. But for a moment, a glimpse of him was back, and it felt good to think that maybe he wasn't so lost after all.

"That was a pretty big fight in there, with Gram, wasn't it?" The awe in her son's voice made her realize that as much as she'd disliked him being present, maybe having him see families working through their conflict had been a valuable lesson for him.

Madison nodded. "It was, but we worked it out. And that's what you're supposed to do when you disagree with someone or when someone hurts you. You have to let it out, and talk about it, rather than letting it fester."

"She admitted she was wrong, and she said she was sorry,"

D.J. said, stopping again to look up at her. "That's what you always try to make me and Faith do, isn't it?"

Madison nodded, then gestured over at a bench in the garden. "Let's go sit."

When they got situated on the bench, D.J. cuddled up to her. "I always thought that when you told me and Faith to work things out, that it was too hard. But maybe, like you kept telling me, I just wasn't giving it enough of a chance."

Madison nodded as she gave her son a big squeeze. "I never said it was easy. I know it was hard for Gram to realize that she'd been wrong. But sometimes you have to decide what's more important to you. The people you love or being right."

D.J. made a face. "I hate it when Faith is right. She's always right, and she acts like such a know it all."

Madison tried not to laugh. Faith had a tendency to be smug when she thought she was one upping her brother.

"Humility is hard, that's for sure. I know I struggle with it."

D.J. gave her strange look. "You? You were always telling Dad you were sorry. He would yell at you, and you would cry and say you were sorry and that you would do better. But he was mean to you, and he never said he was sorry for that."

Dave had never been the kind of person to say he was sorry, ever. He used to tell her that was one of the reasons he didn't respect her, because she apologized. To Dave, it was a sign of weakness, but in her mind it was the right thing to do when you were wrong. However, she recognized now that she often apologized for things she shouldn't have.

D.J. gave her a forlorn look. "He's not coming back, is he?"

Madison let out a long sigh. "I've tried to find him. Hayden has tried to find him. Even his old business partner hasn't been able to figure out where he is. I know it's hard to let him go without being able to ask him why, but I think we have to accept that it's probably not going to happen."

D.J. nodded slowly. "I thought if we could make him proud of us, he would come back. But sometimes I don't know anymore if I want him back. And then I get mad, because he's my Dad, and I should want him back. Dr. Hart says that's normal, but I think it makes me a bad son."

Madison pulled him close to her. "You're not a bad son. I think you're pretty wonderful. And I don't know why your father would give that all up."

D.J. turned away, and she could hear his sniffles. She should be happy that he was finally letting go, but it was hard watching her son's heart break.

"You know that none of this is your fault, right?" she asked.

He sniffled and nodded but didn't turn to look at her. "That's what everyone says, but I know he was mad at me for not making the honor roll the way Faith did. He called me a disappointment, and then all the mean things he said about you, and baby Hope and Faith. No one here says those mean things, not even when we deserve it."

"We all make mistakes," Madison said. "It's like I said in the gift shop. What matters is that we learn from our mistakes and we do better next time. I can tell that you are learning from your mistakes, and everyone has commented about how proud they are of you. I'm proud of you. And if your dad had half a brain, he would be proud of you, too."

D.J. turned to her with a teary-eyed grin. "That's the meanest thing you've ever said about Dad."

Madison smiled. "As a rule, I try not to say anything a bad about him, or anyone else. But anyone who can't see you and your sisters for the wonderful people you are, are clearly not very smart."

D.J. gave her another hug. "And they're not very smart if

they can't see how wonderful you are either," he said. "At first, I didn't want you going out with Wade because I wanted you and Dad to get back together. But now, I don't know if I want that to happen. Dr. Hart said that we need to focus more on the good things in our lives, not the bad ones. I like Dr. Hart. He's teaching me that instead of being mad with all my mad thoughts and being mean to others, I can use those to make my games."

A serious expression crossed his face. "Do you think that's why Dad was so mean to all of us? Maybe he has mad feelings inside of him, and instead of doing something positive, like making a game, he's mean to people?"

Madison hadn't thought of it that way, but she appreciated the wisdom coming from her little boy. She'd thought her divorce was the worst thing that could have possibly happened to them, but as her son jumped off the bench and held his hand out to her, she wondered if maybe it was exactly what they needed.

"I'm not sure. Maybe. Come on. Let's go have some ice cream."

She was surprised she'd gotten so much out of him, but grateful he'd finally opened his heart to her. Hopefully, Wade wouldn't be gone too long on his trip, because she wanted to tell him everything. Not just about her son, but about how much she'd grown during her time here.

As she and her son walked into the house, she felt more positive about her life and was excited for where the next chapter would lead her.

CHAPTER 11

*I*t felt so good to Wade to be back in the fresh air, away from the smog and busyness of the city. Liam had been begging him for years to come back to Silicon Valley, and though it was nice catching up, he knew that this trip had been his last goodbye. He wouldn't return.

As luck would have it, Madison was the first person he saw. He jumped out of his truck and held his arms out to her. "Honey, I'm home."

He'd only been joking, but Madison came running to him. She wrapped her arms around him in a big hug. "And we're so glad you are."

Wow. If this was the welcome home he got, he might have to rethink things and leave a little more often.

But as he looked into her deep brown eyes, he didn't want to leave. He wasn't sure he could ever leave again.

He hugged her back, then released her. "Nice to see you, too. How have things been going since I've been gone?"

Madison's smile warmed him. She seemed almost a completely different person from the one who had arrived only a couple of months ago. Where she'd once been weary and frazzled, she seemed light, happy, and full of hope. Man, he loved this woman.

For a moment, he stilled. He hadn't used that word in relation to her before. He'd known his feelings for her were deep, but this hit him hard.

"Are you all right? Did you forget something?"

Madison's expression of concern jolted him back to reality. He knew she wasn't ready to hear how he felt, so he smiled at her.

"No. I was just thinking how good it is to be back. If I ever say I'm going back there again, please talk me out of it."

"I can understand that. I really love it here. And it makes me so happy to see my kids enjoying themselves as well."

Was it wrong to want to kiss her? Because as she spoke, all he could do was stare at her lips and think about what it would be like to take her in his arms and kiss her finally.

Allie approached, carrying a basket with tiny lavender plants. "Hey guys. Welcome back, Wade."

"Thanks," Wade said. "I was talking to some investors during my trip, and they're keen to come out to the farm and take a look. Later, we can go over some of their ideas. It would bring some much-needed capital into the business, but I don't know if you want that level of growth or to have outsiders involved in the business. Since they approached me, I figured I owed it to you to at least go over their proposal."

Allie stared at him like he'd grown an extra head. "People are interested in investing in my business? It's so weird to think that something everyone called my silly little hobby would get so much attention. My dad even told me last night that he was proud of me. Can you believe that?"

Then she turned to Madison, shaking her head. "It's really crazy to think about how things have changed so dramatically. I overheard Caroline's dad telling a guy at the farmers' market that he thought we were geniuses."

Wade was glad to hear that the rest of the Bigby family was finally coming around in terms of understanding the Bigby grandchildren's drive when it came to saving Bigby Farm. He hadn't heard any rumblings from Enid's children in a long time about wanting to take over the farm and sell it.

He turned his gaze back to Madison. If the other Bigbys could overcome their conflicts and find a way to get along again, he had to believe that there was a similar hope that Madison could find enough healing in her life to give her heart to him.

Allie made an exasperated noise. "You're so pathetic, Wade. You're practically drooling over Madison. Even though I totally agree with Madison for telling Gram not to interfere in our lives, I kind of want both of you to just kiss and get it over with."

Madison blushed, and he couldn't help thinking that it was the most beautiful thing he'd ever seen. Did she have any idea how hard she made it for him to hold back when he wanted to do exactly what Allie suggested?

Allie shook her head. "Well, this box is getting heavy, and whatever's happening in the air between you two, I'm clearly interrupting. So both of you take the rest of the day off, go have a cup of coffee, talk through whatever you need to talk through, and then go find somewhere private to kiss. Because seriously, I don't think I want to see either one of you until you've finally figured it out."

As Allie walked away, he looked at Madison, trying to gauge her feelings. "Do you think kissing would solve what's happening between us?" he asked.

She looked at the ground. "I don't know." Then she looked at him. "To be honest, I don't have a lot of experience in this. I know kissing leads to other things, which, in the past, led to me not being able to think very clearly and making a lot of mistakes. I don't want to make a mistake with you."

He took a step toward her. "So you think about kissing me?"

"Every time I'm with you," she said, taking another step toward him, until they were so close they were almost touching. "So what do we do?"

He took her hands in his. "Maybe we take Allie's advice. We go have a cup of coffee. We talk about the stuff we haven't talked about, and then maybe we find a place where we can kiss in private."

The vulnerability in her eyes as she looked up at him nearly slayed him. "And all we'll do is kiss?"

"I don't want to mess things up between us, either. But I think my heart might explode if I don't get to kiss you soon. I've never felt like this about anyone and, like you, I want to do it right. So yeah, all we'll do is kiss."

She nodded slowly. "Okay. Let me just go tell Gram we're leaving, and make sure she's okay with the kids."

He was glad they'd been standing in the middle of the driveway, and not anywhere where anyone could hear the conversation, because clearly, by the way Enid stepped out of the back door when Madison approached, she'd been watching through the window. He chuckled and shook his head slowly. No wonder Allie had told them to go somewhere private to kiss. The way the Bigbys were, they'd probably pull up a chair and pop some popcorn for the event.

They held hands but didn't talk on the drive to town. Based on how Madison kept looking down and biting her lip, he could tell she was deep in thought over what to say. Fighting between doing the right thing for her kids and following her heart. He didn't think they were mutually exclusive, but he also knew that the timing was important. Which meant he needed to tell her about his trip to Silicon

Valley. And he needed to tell her about his money. But how?

The Beanery was empty when they arrived, a nice lull in the week day between the lunch time and after work crowd. He ordered their coffee, then found them a quiet table in a corner where they wouldn't be disturbed.

Her hand was shaking when he took it.

"You don't have to be scared. I care about you, and I'm not trying to push you into anything you're not ready for. I know we talked about kissing later but if you're not ready, we don't have to. We don't even have to talk about this, if you don't want. I'm willing to wait for whenever you're ready."

It wasn't exactly a lie, because he was willing. But as he said the words, he prayed it wouldn't be a long one.

"I know. I just want to do things right this time. There's a lot more at stake than two crazy kids who think they're in love."

"D.J., Faith, and Hope are just as much of a priority to me. I would never hurt them."

Madison nodded slowly. "I'm still scared of ruining their lives."

He squeezed her hand. "I'm afraid of the same thing."

He smiled at her, wondering where to start, wondering how to talk about things he never talked about.

"My dad died when I was little," he finally said. "Looking back, I don't remember much of it, and as I've tried relating to D.J., and his sadness at his loss of his father, I don't remember how it felt. Maybe because my dad died, instead of just leaving, I had more closure."

A sympathetic expression crossed her face as she gave his hand a squeeze. "It still must have been hard for you to grow up without a dad," she said. "I hated the fact that my dad was dead. Not having a father in your life is hard, which is why

I'm trying to be understanding of my kids. I know it's not the same, but it's still a loss."

He nodded. "After my dad died, there was one guy my mom was getting serious with, but I walked in on him yelling at my mom, so I stepped in. He slapped me so hard, it sent me flying across the room."

Madison gasped, and he squeezed her hands and smiled. "It's okay. Even though that sounds like a horrible thing, and it was, it scared my mom. She threw him out and told him to never come back again. After that, she didn't date anymore. I asked her about it, years later, and told her she should find someone. But she told me she was looking for a man for all the wrong reasons, and what happened that day had made her rethink a lot of her motivations. She told me she'd rather be alone than be with anyone who couldn't love her son as much as she did."

He wasn't the sort of man to cry, but tears sprang to his eyes at the memory.

Wade looked up at Madison. "That's why I understand your need to do the right thing. I do love your children and will love them like my own. Even if you and I end up having more children together, I promise that your children will have nothing to fear from me."

Madison looked thoughtful for a moment. "It might be a little premature, considering we haven't even kissed yet, but I have been thinking about it after what Gram said about us having babies. I honestly don't know if I want more children. How would you feel if I decided I didn't want more?"

He thought for a moment, trying to picture what his life would be like without biological children. Until he'd met Madison, he hadn't thought that he'd have any at all.

"Before I met you, I was perfectly happy being alone. The Bigbys were my family. As I've mentioned, my mother is so deep in her own world, she doesn't know who I am anymore.

I visit her out of obligation, but the person she was doesn't exist anymore."

"But you still visit her?"

He nodded. "Almost every time I go to town alone. Sometimes she's angry and violent, and I never know how she's going to be from one day to the next, so I don't want others to have to deal with it."

She gave him a smile, one of the many that had been directed at him that day, and it was like much-needed sunshine after a rainy spell. Those days in Silicon Valley without her, he genuinely missed her presence. It wasn't just the comfort of fresh air in the farm, but of her.

"I'd like to meet her someday," Madison said.

A group of teenagers walked in, laughing, giggling, and being a little bit rowdy. It was nothing inappropriate, but it felt weird to have that around him when there were so many heavier issues to deal with.

He stood and held his hand out to her. "We can go now, if you like. No one's ever asked to meet her before, and even though it will mean nothing to her, it means the world to me that you're willing."

They drove the short distance to Retro Village, and the nurse at the memory care unit gave him a warm smile. "How was your trip? She had some bad days while you were gone, but today's been a very good one. She mentioned you by name."

Then she laughed. "But we'll see if she recognizes you without the beard."

She led them down the corridor and into his mother's room. She was sitting in her chair, looking out her window, and didn't turn around when they arrived.

"Laverne? Look who's come to visit you. Your son, Wade, and he's brought a rather lovely young lady with him."

His mother turned, the blank expression he'd long been

familiar with on her face. "Wade? He's away at school. He shouldn't be taking time away from his studies."

But she stood anyway. "I'll talk him out of this foolishness and send him on his way. He's going to do great things in his life, mark my words."

She'd told him that his whole life, and he used to wonder if she just said those things because she was his mother. But hearing them in her dementia, he knew it was something she believed deeply to her core.

As she got closer to them, she stopped. "George? What are you doing here? You died twenty years ago. With a Bigby girl? Which one are you? All you Bigbys look exactly alike, with that funny nose of yours."

The cousins all looked so different, Wade didn't understand his mother's words. And, as he glanced at Madison's nose, he couldn't see anything funny about it.

His mother looked down at her hands. "But you're still young, and I'm old. Does this mean I'm dead? I always thought we would get our young bodies back, but I guess I was wrong. It's strange, being dead, because that horrid nurse who makes me take the horse pills is here, too." Then she stopped. "I'm going crazy, aren't I? That's why you're not answering me, isn't it, George?"

Wade took a step toward her. "It's me, Wade. You're not dead, and you're not seeing my father. I've brought someone to meet you, and you're right about her being a Bigby. She's Enid's granddaughter, Madison."

His mother acted like she hadn't heard him. "Well, what are you doing here? You're supposed to be in school. I told you that an education is the most important thing you can do to better yourself. You're going to make something of yourself, so you have to get a good education. Do you hear me?"

"Mom, I did. I went to MIT, remember?"

"Of course I know you go to MIT. I just got a letter from you last week."

If he argued with her, she would only get combative. So he smiled and nodded. "That's right. I just wanted you to meet my good friend, Madison."

His mother turned her attention back to Madison, looking her up and down. "You're not thinking you're going to get yourself knocked up by him and sponge off of him for the rest of your life, are you? Women have a sense about men who are going to be successful, and they like to sink their claws into them when they can."

He winced at his mother's words, knowing it was sort of what happened to Madison in college. He didn't think she'd done it in a mercenary way, but based on the expression on her face, she'd probably been accused of it.

Madison quickly regained her composure and smiled at his mom. "Actually, I have no intention of sponging off your son. I'm a manager of an up-and-coming boutique, and I love the independence it gives me. I have no intention of ever relying on a man to support me."

His mother smiled and gestured to a chair next to the one she'd vacated. "I like you. A little too much Bigby in you, but I don't suppose that's a bad thing. I hear they're all doing quite well for themselves, except for Enid, God love her. But she's always been a little crazy. Crazy but harmless. I don't have anything against her, you understand."

Madison went and sat with his mother, and he followed, standing beside her. But his mother waved him off. "Go study. You've got finals coming up, and I won't have you doing poorly. You might lose your scholarship, and then what? You'll be back here working in some dead-end job you hate, and I won't have that for you.

He smiled as he watched his mother pull out the box of chocolates he'd given her on his last visit and offer some to

Madison. "My son sent these to me all the way from MIT. Don't you think he's considerate, sending me chocolates when he has so many more important things to focus on? But you know, he never forgets about me. Every week, I get a letter from him, and he usually includes a nice treat, like these chocolates."

She leaned in to Madison. "Can I tell you a secret?"

Madison nodded.

"I'm dying. They say I'm just fine, but would I be in this place if I wasn't dying?" .

Then his mother smiled softly. "It's okay though, because then I'll be back with George. I miss him. For a while, I tried to replace him, but there will never be anyone for me but George. Do you love my son like that?"

He held his breath as Madison nodded slowly. "He's the best man I know."

It wasn't an admission of love, but the warmth in her expression gave him hope that it could be, someday.

"Good. But you make sure she finishes school. He keeps talking nonsense about coming home to help me, and I won't have it. He's got to get an education."

His mother let out a long sigh. "I just know that if George had gone and gotten an education instead of staying home to help his mother run the farm after his father died, he would still be with us today. But he couldn't bear for his mother to lose the family farm, and it killed him, working full-time at the factory, then coming back to work on the farm. I think that's why he died so young. They say it was a bad heart, but I think it was too much work. Maybe I should have gotten rid of the farm, so Wade isn't tempted to come back and bury himself there. But George loved it so much, and I couldn't bear to part with it. If he was willing to die to save it, how can I get rid of it? You'll make sure Wade doesn't work too hard, won't you?"

He'd never heard any of these things from his mother before. And even though it was tempting to pass them off as the delusional ramblings of an old woman, he knew she was telling the truth. She sensed that Madison was someone important to him, and that she wanted to pass on her wisdom and encouragement to make sure Wade was taken care of. She might think herself in the wrong time, but the rest was true.

Madison reached forward and gave his mother a hug. "Of course I will. I would do anything for your son."

His throat tightened as his mother hugged her back. "Be good to him. He deserves to be loved."

"I will," Madison said as she pulled away.

His mother nodded. "I know. You're a Bigby. The heart of a Bigby is a loving and compassionate heart, and it's exactly what my son needs."

Then his mother stood. "Now go. I'm tired. Why are you people bothering me? You need to leave now."

Madison stood and nodded. "Yes. It's getting late. Do you want me to help get you settled?"

"No. Go." She turned and looked at Wade. "And what are you still doing here? I told you to study. If you lose your scholarship, it will be the end of everything we've worked so hard for."

He nodded as he stepped forward and held out his arms. "I'm going to go do that right now."

His mother let him hug her, and then she pushed him away. It was the longest visit they'd had, and one of the most productive. He could see tears in Madison's eyes as he took her hand and led her out of the room. They didn't speak until they got to his truck.

"I wasn't expecting it to be so intense," Madison said. "That was something else. I've never been around someone like that before."

"I'm sorry," he said. "I hope it wasn't too disturbing."

She shook her head. "No. It's clear she really loves you, and just wants the best for you. You mentioned once that you felt bad for the years when you were working so hard and didn't spend time with her. I don't think she minded. I think that's what she wanted."

He smiled as she scooted next to him. "I agree. It's just hard, seeing her like this."

Madison took his hand. "I don't think your mother has any hard feelings. She just wants you to be happy and taken care of, which is all I want for my children."

He looked down at her and wanted nothing more than to take her in his arms and never let go. She brought a light and understanding to him that made his life make sense.

She gave him a shy smile. "You're thinking about kissing again, aren't you?"

He laughed. "I wasn't until you said it, but now—"

Before he could finish the sentence, she reached up and kissed him. A gentle kiss, but so electric it sent shockwaves rippling through his body. When he moved to deepen the kiss, she pulled away.

"Let's not push it," she said. "I knew I'd like it, but not how much."

Tears filled her eyes as she looked back at him. "I wasn't expecting to fall in love. But I'm scared, because I don't know what I'm doing, and yet, it's happening anyway."

He brushed the tears away from her cheeks. Maybe they were closer to finding happiness together than he'd thought. "And you think I'm an expert on falling in love? You might have gone a little wild in college, but I was the opposite. I was so afraid of messing up and losing my scholarship that I worked and studied twice as hard as everyone else I knew. When I moved to Silicon Valley and started working, I would date casually, but I never fell in love with any of them. I spent most of my dates wondering how soon I could drop the girl off without seeming rude, so I could get back to work."

Then he looked at her. "Loving you is different. When I'm with you, I just want to be with you. And not just so we can kiss and do other things, but because I like your company. I feel safe with you because you love me for who I am."

Madison nodded. "With Dave, I was as worried about saying or doing the wrong thing because he'd see through me and I would mess it all up. I don't feel that way when I'm with you, so why am I scared?"

He bent and kissed her again, deliberately keeping it gentle and easy, but hoping she felt the depth of love that he felt for her.

This time, he pulled away first. When she looked up at him, breathless, he smiled.

"Because it doesn't feel like that for everyone. Can you honestly tell me, that in your most heated college moments with Dave, that any of it ever felt remotely close to this?"

Maybe he shouldn't have said anything, because what if it had been? He didn't think so, but he was relieved when she shook her head.

"I was scared, but in a different way. I didn't want to disappoint him. But I know I will never disappoint you. You love and accept me for who I am, so I don't know why I'm scared, except that I don't want to hurt my kids."

He brushed the hair away from her cheek. "I read somewhere that excitement and fear feel the same way sometimes. But let's not push it. We can head home, and you can tell Allie that we finally kissed, have a nice giggle, and we'll come back to this another time."

There was still so much he had to say to her, but something in him told him they both needed a breather.

She grinned. "Talking, or the kissing?"

He couldn't help planting a kiss on her forehead. "How about both?"

On the drive home, they talked about mundane things, as Madison caught him up on what happened on the farm while he was gone. Nothing of significance, but it felt good to bring things back to normal.

When they pulled into the driveway, a brand-new sports car was parked in front of the house. As they slowed to see the man getting out, Madison gasped.

"What's wrong?" Wade asked, an uneasy feeling in his gut.

Madison turned to him, wide-eyed. "Dave's here."

CHAPTER 12

"What are you doing here?" Madison stared at Dave and tried not to gag at the scent of his cologne.

"Nice to see you, too, babe." He pulled her into his arms and planted a kiss on her lips.

She shoved him away. "We're divorced, remember? You can't show up and kiss me anytime you want."

He looked like a puppy dog that had just been kicked, but she reminded herself that people had taken in wolves and coyotes, thinking they were puppies, then realizing at the worst possible time, they were actually wild animals.

"I'm sorry," he said. "I missed you."

"Missed me? No one's heard for you in months. How about calling first?"

Dave gave a casual shrug, like she was mad at him over a trivial matter. "I might have gone a little crazy there for a minute."

She stared at him. "A minute? Your kids haven't heard from you in almost nine months, and the best you can say is you went crazy for a minute?"

He didn't even have the nerve to look sorry. Instead, he looked at her with a greedy expression on his face. "Let's leave them out of this for a while. You're looking good. Have you been working out? What diet are you on? If you lose a few more pounds, you'll be as fine as the day I met you."

Had she really fallen for this guy? Because right now, which she wanted to do was punch him. Not out of revenge, but because his words were just so offensive to her that she couldn't comprehend why he would think it was okay to talk to her like that.

Wade stepped in beside her. "She doesn't need to lose a few pounds. If you ask me, she's perfect the way she is, and she was beautiful even before she lost any weight."

Dave eyed him as if he were measuring him up. "And just who are you? I don't think I like the way you're talking about my wife."

"Ex-wife," Wade said. "I've seen the divorce papers as well as the documents that say you owe her quite a bit of money in back support and alimony." Then he pointed at the sports car. "So could you please explain why you're driving that when your kids have school fees that need to be paid?"

It was sweet of Wade to be so defensive about the school fees, and she wanted to interrupt to say that she had them covered. She'd paid them the day before, and it felt good to pay them with money she'd earned herself. And even though she was very well prepared to tell Dave that she was doing just fine on her own, it was nice watching him squirm over the fact that he'd left her high and dry.

"Don't worry," Dave said. "I've got it covered. I'm taking them back home and enrolling them in their old school."

Madison stared at him. "I hate to break it to you, but number one, this is their home now. And number two, I had to have a very uncomfortable conversation with the head-master over the fact that we couldn't pay last semester's fees.

One more bill that I still have to pay because you thought it would be fun to charge up all the credit cards and leave the bank account empty while you went off to find yourself."

If he had looked regretful or truly sorry, Madison might have backed off. But he just stood there, looking like she was in the wrong for calling him out.

"I'll take care of it. Let's just all go home, where we can talk it out."

"Home?" How stupid was he? "You mean the one that got foreclosed on? I'm curious where you think home is now, because after losing everything, I moved in with my grandmother and I'm pretty sure she's not going to welcome you here."

Dave looked flabbergasted. "You have a grandmother?"

"Maybe, if you'd been in my life over the past several months, you would know that I reconnected with my father's side of the family. Or maybe, if you'd actually read any of the emails your son sent you, you'd know what was going on."

Before he had time to come up with a response, which would've probably been just as stupid as every other thing that had come out of his mouth, another car pulled into the driveway.

Her mother stepped out of the car.

Madison couldn't even comprehend what this was all about. "Mom. What are you doing here?"

Her mother smiled as she walked over to Madison and gave her a hug. "I've missed you. Besides, Dave called. He said you guys were working things out and asked me to cosign on a loan to help him get his business back on his feet while he waits for a payout on a business venture. Isn't it terrible how his business partner stole all that money from him?"

This had to be some kind of weird nightmare. She gestured at the sports car Dave was driving. "Does that look like he has no money? Let's get a few things straight. I am never getting back together with Dave. Never. Not only did he abandon me and our children to go find himself with some yoga instructor he ran off to India with, he left me completely penniless. There was no money in the bank account, all the credit cards were maxed out, and our house was under foreclosure. As for his business partner stealing all his money, you might want to check those facts. If it weren't for my cousin's husband being a lawyer, I'd be paying off a lawsuit because it was actually Dave who took all the money."

"Now wait just a second," Dave said. "That's not true."

Madison stared at him. "No. It is true. And I'm tired of you lying to everyone about it. Especially me." Then she turned and looked at her mother. " I'm sorry that you think I've done all these horrible things. But I can guarantee that most of what Dave had told you is a lie. If you want supporting evidence, I'm happy to provide it. Not only did he saddle me with a bunch of debt, but he hasn't paid a dime of child support or alimony. When I called you asking for help, it was because I had nothing. You told me I made my bed and I had to lie in it. But now he comes running back, and you're more than happy to help him out."

Madison looked behind her intending to gesture at the house, but realized that her cousins and Gram had come out, along with the children. Ordinarily, she wouldn't have said anything in front of the kids, but she was tired of the lies, and based on her conversations over the past few days with them, she knew that they saw their father for who he was.

"Mom, he lied to all of us. When I had nowhere else to go and no other options, my Bigby relatives took me in. Over the years, you've told me that they're horrible people and I'm better off without them. But I'm telling you that I can't imagine my life without them. So if you're here to try to save my marriage, you need to get back in your car and go home."

D.J. and Faith ran over to her and she put her arms

around them. "But if you're here to have a relationship with me and the kids, I know Gram is more than willing to bury the hatchet and we would love for you to be a part of our lives."

Then she turned her attention back to Dave. "As for you, I am more than happy to co-parent with you in an equitable way as lined out in our divorce agreement. You are entitled to visitation, but I'm entitled to making sure their well-being comes first. So, what do you have to say to your children after ignoring them for the past nine months?"

Dave opened his mouth then closed it.

D.J. pulled away from her, then walked up to his dad. "I thought the day you came back would be the happiest day of my life. But you didn't even ask her how we were. You didn't even say you read my emails. Why are you even here?"

She was proud of the way her son stood up to his father, but she was even more proud when Faith joined him and put her arm around her brother.

"It's complicated," Dave said. "Your mom hasn't given me a chance to explain."

"Then explain," D.J. said.

Dave shifted uncomfortably. "It's a grown-up conversation. I need to talk to her alone."

Madison didn't need to hear his explanation anymore. She was done with him and didn't care for her sake. But the kids, they needed him to man up.

"Your children need to hear it too," she said.

Dave looked like a child who'd been caught sneaking sweets. But she could see the flash of anger in his eyes at the fact that she was finally standing up to him. Even though her family hadn't said anything, having them standing behind her gave Madison the strength to let Dave know to his face that his behavior wasn't okay.

"I'm sorry," Dave said. "Is that what you want to hear? You

think it's easy to come back and admit when you've messed up?"

That was probably the most sincere thing he'd said this whole time. "So you admit that you made a mistake?" Madison asked.

Dave took a step forward. "The biggest of my life."

His voice caught as he spoke, and Madison believed him. But that didn't mean she was going to welcome him back, either.

"And what brought on this change of heart?" she asked.

"Like I said, I missed you," he said.

Madison could hear Gram behind her, snorting. Allie nudged her and told her to hush, but Madison fully agreed with Gram.

"What's with this sudden realization?" Madison asked.

Even though she really didn't care anymore about him cheating, she couldn't help adding, "Things with your new girlfriend didn't work out?"

He made a disgusted noise. "She got pregnant, can you believe that? She claims it's mine, but how am I supposed to believe her? We weren't exclusive. It was one of those free love kind of places. For all I know that kid's father could be anyone. I've already got three brats to support. I'm not adding one more."

She hated to break it to him that it didn't actually work that way, and if he was this baby's father, he would be responsible for it as well, but he'd already dug himself a big enough grave. Did he understand what he'd just said in front of his children?

Madison glared at him. "Maybe we shouldn't have this discussion in front of the kids after all." She turned and looked at Allie. "Would you mind taking them somewhere where they can't hear? I'm starting to think that it's probably inappropriate for their ears."

Allie groaned. "But it's just getting interesting. I wanted to see how the scumbag jerk talked himself out of this one."

"I want to stay," D.J. said.

"Yeah," Dave said. "I have every right to see my kids if I want to. It's in the divorce papers."

Madison nodded. "You're absolutely right. I'm glad to see you taking interest in your children's lives. I hope you'll take an equal amount of interest in catching up on all the back child support you owe. Even though I've caught up on their school fees, I haven't bought school clothes yet, or their school supplies. Perhaps you'd like to take care of that."

Dave shifted uneasily. "That was always your job."

Madison smiled at him. "Yes, but we're co-parenting now. Which means we work together for the benefit of our children, and we share in the responsibility of raising them."

Dave rolled his eyes. "Now you sound just like her. I provide for my family, that should be plenty."

Clearly Dave was on another planet. "When can I expect my support check then?" Madison asked.

Dave looked even more nervous. Did he really expect that he could just waltz back into their lives and start where he'd left off? Without taking any responsibility?

"It's coming," he said. "I just need some signatures on the papers."

At least she finally knew what he was really here for. She wished he could've just come out and said it, but that was never Dave's style.

"What papers?" she asked.

Dave shifted nervously. "You remember our investment company?"

"You mean the one your business partner was going to sue me over because you'd stolen all the money?"

Dave shifted uneasily. "It was a misunderstanding. These papers will clear it up."

Whatever it was, it was bound to be a scam. But now that she had a lawyer in her back pocket, she wasn't going to be fooled again.

"Great. Why don't you leave them here with me, and I'll take a look at them while you spend some time with your children? As I've mentioned, the only relationship with you I'm interested in is one where we both successfully co-parent our children. Let me get Hope's car seat for you, and you can take the kids for a ride. There is a great ice cream shop in town that we all love, and it would be a great place for you to spend some time catching up."

Dave glared at her. "So I can only spend time with them on your terms? What if I want to take them someplace else? I saw an amusement park outside Twin Falls that I think they'll love."

He was being contrary, probably to get her to say no, but she smiled at him. "That sounds like a lot of fun. I know the place you're talking about. The last time we went to Twin Falls, D.J. asked if we could go, but it wasn't possible."

Dave shifted nervously. She'd called his bluff, and he knew it. Finally, he said, "All right. I'll take them. It will be good to reconnect with my children."

She could feel Wade's eyes on her throughout the conversation, and as she helped Dave strap the car seat into his sports car, she could feel Wade silently pleading with her not to let the children go with him. But he'd been the one to encourage D.J. in thinking that his dad would come home someday, and now that Dave was here, he was seeing for himself what it was like.

When Dave left with the children, Madison handed the papers he'd wanted her to sign to Hayden. "Now tell me what they say."

Hayden scanned the papers. "Apparently one of the start-ups your husband's company invested in is being bought out. It's a nice price. If the deal goes through, your company's share would be significant. Split between all the corporate partners, it would give you a nice nest egg." Then he stopped.

"What?" Madison asked. "It's too good to be true, isn't it?"

~

WADE HATED the expression on Hayden's face as the other man turned to him.

"I don't know, Wade. Is it?"

He could feel the weight of Madison's gaze on him, trying to figure out what was going on.

"Please tell me you didn't do what I think you did." Hayden asked Wade.

Wade shrugged. "Someone had to draw him out."

"I thought you agreed not to meddle," Allie said.

"What's going on?" Madison asked.

Wade hated the way Madison's cousins made him sound guilty of a crime when he'd just been trying to help. Especially because his idea had worked. Dave had come out of hiding to collect what he thought was a big payday. The kids could get whatever closure they needed to, and maybe he and Madison could finally move on with their lives together.

Wade shrugged. "It was nothing. When I was looking at the papers Hayden had about Dave, I recognized the name of one of the companies he'd invested in. It was one my friend Liam thought had a lot of potential in the tech world. I looked into it, and I realized that if I helped Liam buy out this company, the other investors would get their money back. It was a big enough investment that I knew it would be a significant payday for Madison. At least she'd have money for the kids. Maybe put some aside for college since all the paperwork indicated that Dave had even drained their college funds. It seemed like the right thing to do."

Madison stared at him. "You bought out the company?"

He nodded. "I wouldn't have done it if it wasn't a good deal. Like I said, Liam had been talking to me about it for months, saying he thought it had a lot of potential. In the end, it'll be a win-win. I really believe in this technology they're developing, and it helps you out. What's wrong with that?"

He didn't expect the full force of Madison's fury loosed upon him. She hadn't even been this mad at Dave.

"Well, for starters, you could have talked to me about it. Who wanted your involvement? And where'd you get the money, anyway?"

Wade ignored Allie's I told you so look and sighed as he looked over at Madison. "There might be a few things about me you don't know."

"A few?"

Enid clapped her hands. "All right everyone, show's over. You all wanted me to stop interfering, so we all need to butt out. Let's go inside and leave these two to duke it out by themselves."

He couldn't believe Enid chose now to stop meddling.

But maybe, with Madison's anger turned on him, he didn't need everyone to witness the lashing he didn't think he deserved.

"I'm sorry," he said. "That was one of the things I intended to talk to you about today, but when we went to visit my mom, I got distracted."

Madison looked at him like she thought he was making up the kind of excuse Dave would. But he wasn't Dave, and he had good reasons for everything. If Madison would be willing to hear him out.

"I know everyone thinks that I moved back home because I got burned out. And in a way, that's true. But what I didn't put out there for everyone to know is that I made a lot of money when I sold my company. Enough that I never have to work again. Most of my money, I keep in a charitable trust, where I donate to worthy causes as they arise. But I also like to stay on the lookout for up-and-coming startups in need of a little investment to get going. If it hadn't been for someone believing in me when I got my start, I wouldn't be where I am today. My friend Liam keeps an eye out and lets me know of ones that hold promise."

He let out a long sigh. "I don't like telling people about my money, because back when I was in Silicon Valley, it seemed like that was all people were interested in me for. And I didn't really know how to tell you, oh by the way, I'm rich. You've got to understand, I might have money, but I'm living the way I want to. I'm perfectly happy living a minimalist lifestyle."

"And when were you planning on telling me you had all this money?" Madison asked, glaring at him.

"Soon. Today, had we not..."

He didn't think it would take help his case to say that he'd been about to tell her when she kissed him.

"The day didn't exactly go as planned, as you recall. By the time we got back, your ex was here, and everything exploded."

Madison nodded slowly. "And why had you decided to tell me?"

He let out a long sigh. "Because I finally thought we were getting a relationship on track. I didn't want there to be any secrets between us. You yourself said that you were scared about jumping into a relationship. Don't you think, that with all those years of women throwing themselves at me because they knew I was loaded, I might be a little hesitant to tell someone with over a hundred thousand dollars in credit card debt that hey, by the way, I'm rich?"

"So you were afraid to trust me?"

Great. That hadn't come out how he meant it. "In the beginning, yes. I'm afraid to tell anyone how much money I have. The Bigbys suspect, but they have no idea exactly how much it is. There is literally no one in the entire world who knows exactly how much money I have except for me."

She squared her shoulders and looked him in the eye. "How much?"

Wade closed his eyes and took a deep breath. It wasn't that the money meant anything to him, it was more the way people treated him because of it. But he'd told her he trusted her with it, and now he had to do so.

"Somewhere in the neighborhood of a couple billion, give or take," he said, watching the shock register on her face. It felt weird, saying it out loud, especially because he'd spent so long hiding it.

"It doesn't even seem like a real number," she said. "You really sold your company for that much money?"

Wade shrugged, trying to move past the weirdness of what seemed like an impossibly large number. "Not exactly. I sold it for just under a billion, but you can't just let money like that sit around in the bank, so I invested some of it. I'm always careful to invest only in things I believe in, and I give a lot to charity. But a lot of the startups that I've invested in have done well for themselves. They make money, so I end up making money. Liam jokingly tells me that I know how to pick a winner. But I'm not trying to get richer. I meant it when I said I just want to give a hand up to people like I'd been. But I also don't want to give a handout."

Madison stared at him for a moment. "If you don't want the money, why don't you give it all away?"

He let out a long sigh. "Because. I tried that. If you give away too much of a large sum to a charity, then you get all this attention for being a generous benefactor. They put your name on plaques and stuff, even when you say you want to be anonymous. More than that, then you get all kinds of people coming out of the woodwork, begging for money. I worked hard for what I got, and I don't want to give it to someone who's just going to waste it. I want to do real good with my money, not just throw it at things without a plan."

She was starting to look calmer, and he hoped that it meant she was starting to understand. But they hadn't covered his interference with her ex-husband, and he wasn't sure how to answer for it. The betrayal on her face had been real, and from the way Hayden and Allie had looked at him, Wade knew he should have talked it over with her before he acted.

He gestured toward the lavender fields. "Can we take a walk? I think better when I'm moving, and I know I owe you an explanation for what I did."

Madison nodded slowly, but when he held his hand out to her, she refused to take it. "I'm still mad at you, and I don't know if this is something we can work through."

He nodded as they made their way toward one of the paths that meandered through the lavender field separating Bigby Farm from his old place.

"When I saw that his business partner was suing you, I lost it. It seemed so unjust that all these people were suffering, and Dave was getting off scot-free. I don't think his partner was suing you because he wanted to hurt you. I think he was just as desperate as you'd been, and he thought that maybe a lawsuit would draw Dave out. But it's obvious consequences don't motivate Dave, just like they don't motivate D.J. As Dave's consequences get bigger and bigger, he just runs farther and farther. So, I figured, if Dave thought he was getting a big payout, he'd show up for that, and then maybe everyone could get some closure."

He stopped when the path split, one direction going to

the house Allie now occupied, and the other going toward his tiny house.

"Which way do you want to go? If it makes you feel safer, we could go to Allie's." He looked at her, trying to read her expression. "But you've never been to my tiny house, and I would love to show it to you. Maybe if you saw it, and how I lived, you would understand a little more about me. I promise I won't try to kiss you or anything. I just thought, that if I laid everything bare to you, you would know that I never intended to hurt you."

She nodded and turned in the direction of his house. "I'll admit, I've been curious about your tiny house. You're very private about it, about a lot of things, and I really thought that you were finally opening up to me by letting me meet your mother."

He walked in front of her, then stopped. "Don't you get it? I've been more open with you than anyone else in my life."

Her expression softened as she nodded. "Everyone says you're pretty private," she said. "But the way you've been talking to me, about our future, you owe to me to tell me everything."

Some of the heaviness in his heart lifted. "Does that mean there's a chance you'll forgive me?"

Madison shrugged. "I can't answer that."

They walked in silence to his tiny house, which was hidden in the grove of trees along the creek. It was deep enough on his property that no one would've been able to see it from the street even if the trees hadn't been there, but he liked that they gave him additional privacy.

"Here it is," he said. "I built it myself."

He opened the door and led her inside. He looked around at the utilitarian space, wondering what she would think of it. It had a basic kitchen, a table that had two chairs, but only because the table came with it, some storage space, and a very basic bathroom with a composting toilet, sink, and shower. There was a ladder that led up to the loft where his bed was, but even that was basic.

"There's nothing to indicate the personality of who lives here," Madison said. "The tiny houses Hayden and Caroline built for the guests are better appointed than this."

Wade pulled out one of the chairs from his table and offered her a seat, then he sat in the other one.

"I don't need all that junk. I've had it, and it didn't make me any happier."

He gestured to the collage frame on his wall. "Those are the things that are important to me."

He got up and pointed to a picture. "That one is my mom and dad on their wedding day." He smiled as he remembered the way his mother had been talking about being with him again.

Madison must have remembered the same thing, because she smiled too, giving him the encouragement to explain the rest of the pictures in the frame.

Finally, he opened his cupboard door, where he hung some pictures her kids had made for him. "They kept falling off my fridge, so I wanted to keep them safe. I treasure them."

Madison came to stand beside him. "Thanks for sharing your treasures with me.

"Does that mean you forgive me?" he asked.

Madison wrapped her arms around him and squeezed him tight. "I want to," she whispered. "But I'm really hurt by the way you went behind my back, and I don't know if I can trust you again."

She stood on tiptoe and kissed his cheek, then she turned and let herself out of his tiny house.

Maybe he'd been wrong in thinking that he wanted someone to love him for who he was. He'd shown Madison the entirety of his heart, but it hadn't been enough. But as he saw her walking back down the path, he raced out after her.

"Wait."

She stopped and turned. "Why?"

He took a deep breath. "There's one more thing I haven't shown you. One more secret. I didn't tell you, because I thought you would think it was premature. But if you want to know everything, let me show you this one last thing."

She nodded as he led her back into his tiny house. He pulled out the paper he spent every night working on. Then he rolled it out on the table for her.

"I figured, if we ever got married, you'd want something different than the tiny house." He gestured around the interior. "I'm not so stupid as to think that the kids would be happy in here. But I didn't want to kick Allie out of my mom's house, because she's really happy there and she's made it a home for her and Cole."

He gestured to an area on the map of his property. "That corner is a nice piece of land, right along the road. I put in an application with the county to put in a driveway there. I figured we could build something new. Together."

He grabbed the folder he kept by the table and opened it for her. "I know you probably want a say in what our future house would look like, but I've been doodling and drawing up plans. I was going to give them to you as a present and let you make any changes you wanted, but this is what I had in mind."

He spread the plans out before her, watching as she examined them.

Then she looked up at him. "Baby's room? So you do want a baby."

He shrugged, then looked away. "I just thought you'd look cute pregnant. And I've never held a baby before. I love the kids and all, but I'm sad I didn't get to see them as babies.

But," he looked up at her. "I meant what I said earlier. It's a decision we'd make together. If you don't want more children, we won't have any more. We could turn that room into a guest room or something."

She nodded as she traced the outline of the room. He'd tried to think of everything, but as he watched her going over the plans, he wondered if she thought he was being stupid. He slammed the folder shut.

"I'm sorry. You probably think this is just one more way I was taking over. I'd planned on getting your input, this was just me dreaming."

She covered his hands with hers. "Don't be embarrassed. I like it. Sure, there are things that if it were my house, I would do differently. But you clearly put a lot of thought into this, and into our future together."

Madison pulled the folder out from his hands and opened it again. Then she pointed to the playroom. "You put a lot of thought into making sure this was a good house for everyone."

The weight of her gaze on him made him uneasy. He knew this was a test, and yet he wasn't sure how he was going to pass. This wasn't the sort of thing a person studied for.

"I couldn't tell you how I felt," he said. "Not when you had so much to figure out for yourself. But I thought a lot about what I wanted our lives to look like together."

"Go on," she said. "I meant it when I said 'everything.'"

She put her hands over his again, and their warmth comforted him.

"Like I said, I was going to build a house, so you had a place of your own. But I also wanted you close to your family. I thought it would be nice, on good days, we could just walk to work at Bigby Farm. And on bad days, it's an easy drive. I figured we'd go to work in the mornings, and come home in the evenings, we could do things together as a family. Things like you do at Enid's house now. Only you'd be at our house—with me."

She reached up and touched his cheek gently, softly, and he closed his eyes, enjoying the loving touch, and praying this wasn't the end.

"Thank you," she said. "You've given me a lot to think about."

This time, when she left, he let her go. He'd truly given her everything, and now it was up to her to decide what she wanted.

CHAPTER 13

hen Madison returned to Gram's house, she asked Hayden to draw up paperwork to approve the deal Wade had made to save them, but also to dissolve her partnership with Dave. She hadn't seen the necessity of it with their divorce, because there was nothing left to divide up. And even though she appreciated that this had been Wade's way of drawing him out, she honestly never wanted Dave to have the excuse to do this again. Even though he'd taken the kids, she knew they weren't really what he was here for. At least, with Wade's interference, Dave would be gone for good.

She just hoped the kids were having a good time with him. And maybe, Dave would prove her wrong and step up to be the father they needed.

Allie entered the room and put her arm around Madison. "I'm sorry about Wade. I did tell him not to meddle, but I think he genuinely was trying to help."

"I just wish he didn't keep his feelings to himself so much," Madison said.

Allie nodded. "I think it's the eternal dilemma of men and

women. We never seem to be able to communicate with each other the way we all want. But in Wade's case, I think it's harder. He protects himself a lot, but we've all been kind of amazed at how much he's opened up to you and the kids. He may not say how he feels about you, but it's obvious in all his actions. It doesn't make what he did right, but I really hope you guys find a way to work it out."

The sound of a car pulling in the driveway interrupted their conversation.

Dave wasn't due to be back with the kids yet, but she knew from past experience that he lost patience with them pretty quickly. As she suspected, the kids were getting out of Dave's car, both girls were crying, and D.J. looked about ready to join them

Before Madison could get to the car, D.J. had already unbuckled Hope from her car seat and was carrying her over. He held her out at an odd angle, and when Madison got closer, she could see why.

Hope had thrown up all over herself.

"Oh no. You poor thing. Are you sick, little Hope?"

Dave stomped toward her. "She threw up all over the car. It's not even my car. It's a rental. I can't believe you would send a sick child with me."

Gram rushed out of the house and took Hope from her arms. "I'll take care of her. You deal with this."

Madison glared at Dave. "She was fine when she left. I would never send a sick child out."

She turned to D.J. "What happened?"

Faith gestured at her soggy dress. "We ate too much junk food," she said "Gram was right. Can I go inside and change?"

As she looked at her children, she realized they both had been hit with Hope's tsunami of vomit. Even Dave had a few splotches on his back, but she wasn't going to be kind enough to mention it to him.

"Of course. Go take care of it. I'll get Hope's car seat. She walked over the car and was torn between disgust and the urge to laugh hysterically. Hope had projectile vomited all over the car. She wasn't sure there was a surface that she'd missed. Covering her nose with her shirt, Madison quickly pulled the car seat out of the car and tossed it on the lawn. They could hose it down later.

She stepped away from the car and into an area where she couldn't smell the disaster that had happened.

"So the kids had little junk food, did they?" she asked.

Dave looked at her like she said he felt her comments were more disgusting than the vomit. "They were hungry. We went through the drive through. You used to do it all the time. And then we went to the amusement park and I paid a lot of money for their admission, then bought them popcorn, candy, and even ice cream. They should have been having a great time. But we were there only a short time when Faith said she wanted to go home. I told them no, because we paid to be there, and we were going to have fun. But then Hope went on the swing ride, got off, and threw up everywhere. And everyone was looking at me like I was a bad dad for bringing a sick kid to the amusement park. I tried to explain to them that it was my stupid ex-wife who sent the sick kid, but none of them were very sympathetic."

Wow. Stupid ex-wife. And yet he missed her?

"That's too bad. Did it occur to you that maybe after eating all that junk food and then going on a bunch of rides that she might have an upset stomach?"

"I'm not equipped to handle these things," he said. "I don't know why you let me take them."

Madison smiled at him. "Because I'm trying to cooperatively co-parent with you, and I wouldn't dream of denying you your parental time with your children."

He glared at her. "Whatever. Did you sign the papers?"

Hayden joined them. "Yes, she did. However, we have a few documents we'd like you to sign. The first is a simple dissolution of partnership, so that she will have no part of any of your future business dealings. The second is a copy of your divorce papers, and acknowledgement that you've received them. Also, since you're here, I'd like to know what your intentions are regarding paying your child support and alimony."

Caroline walked around the corner of the house with her mother, Camille, along with Madison's mom. The two women were catching up after so many years apart.

Her mother came around just in time to hear Dave say, "Good luck with that. You're not getting a dime. I'm taking the money from the sale of this deal, along with the money I got from your mother, and I'm going to find myself a nice place to settle down with some cute señorita in Mexico. Preferably one without kids."

Before Madison could address his words, her mother marched up to Dave. "You'd better change your plans, because I called the bank and put a stop payment on the check I gave you. You told me it was to get yours and Madison's business back on track, but clearly that isn't what you're intending to do. I don't like being lied to, and I'm especially upset that you told me so many lies about Madison."

She looked apologetically over at Madison. "I'm really sorry for how I acted about your divorce. Dave had called me and told me that your shopping was out of control, and you'd racked up over hundred thousand dollars in credit card debt. He said he was teaching you a lesson, so that you would stand on your own two feet and I shouldn't help you. But while you were off for a walk with your friend, Hayden showed me the paperwork, proving that the real spending problems were Dave's, and that he'd left you on the hook while he was off getting some poor ignorant girl pregnant. I'm so sorry for having doubted you."

Madison didn't even know how to process her mother's words. But it gave her hope that good could come of the situation.

Her mother shook her head slowly, looking discouraged. "As I thought about the things he told me about your divorce, as well as other things he's said over the years, I've realized that I've missed out on so much because he's been lying to me for years."

Madison put her arms around her mother. "You still have plenty of time. You're welcome here anytime, and now that D.J. and Faith are older, maybe I could send them out to visit you or something."

Her mom smiled. "I'd like that."

Hayden turned to Dave. "I think it goes without saying that you aren't welcome here anymore. Given that today's visit was such a disaster, I'll be filing paperwork with the court to ask that future visits be supervised. Maybe, as you're more comfortable with the children, we can talk about unsupervised visits, but for now, I think it's better for everyone if you're not on your own with them again."

Dave glared at him. "Do whatever you have to do. If I'd wanted visitation, I would have seen them by now. The only reason I came here was to get Madison to sign those papers. I thought she'd be more difficult about it." He looked down at his shoes. "And I'm sending you a bill for my cleaning expenses."

Hayden laughed. "Good luck with that one. Your kid, your responsibility."

Dave stomped off to his car and Madison went inside to check on the children. Hope had just come out of the bath and was smelling a lot better.

Madison gathered her baby up and snuggled her close. "Mommy loves you."

Hope rested her head on her chest. "I love you too."

Her daughter's baby voice warmed her heart, and she thought about how she'd once wanted a dozen kids running around laughing and playing. She thought Dave had shared that dream, but she'd been wrong. If only he'd just had the guts to tell her the truth back then, it would have saved them all a lot of heartache.

As she bent to kiss the wet head of her delightful little girl, she knew she wouldn't have done it any differently. She might've left him a sooner, but she didn't regret her three children for anything. She thought to Wade and his misguided attempt at saving her.

He hadn't told her the truth at first, but when she asked him about it, she he'd been open, even to the point of sharing pieces of his heart that was probably hard for him to do so. He fully expected her to reject him, and still, he told her of his most secret dreams. And as she rocked her little girl in the chair that had rocked generations of Bigbys, she couldn't help thinking that it would be awfully nice to add a few more.

D.J. came down the stairs, having taken a shower upstairs, while Faith came out of the downstairs bath.

"I heard what he said," D.J. said. "The bathroom window was open, and I could hear everything. We don't have to see him again, do we?"

Madison shook her head. "Not if you don't want to. Hayden is filing some paperwork with the courts to limit his access, so if he comes around again, we can send him on his way."

D.J. looked at her longingly. "I'll bet you wish we were never born, don't you?"

Even though she was already holding Hope, she patted her lap. "Come on guys, sit."

She shifted so she had her arms around all three children and said, "You three are the best things that have ever happened to me. And I was just thinking that everything we've gone through has been worth it because I have you guys. I'm sorry that I picked such a bad guy to be a dad, but hopefully, the next time around, I'll choose someone better."

D.J. looked up at her and smiled. "Can it be Wade? I think he really loves you, and he treats us all way better than Dad ever did. Plus, he's taught me a lot of cool things, and like I told you the other day, even when I was a jerk, he never treated me the way Dad did."

Faith nodded. "He doesn't say we need to lose weight to be pretty. And he always listens to me when I come up to him to tell him my stories. I hope you do marry Wade, because I think he would be a good dad."

Maybe it hadn't been such a bad thing that her kids had seen their father for who he really was. Even though D.J. was beginning to get the picture for himself, witnessing it firsthand erased any doubt that might have lingered in his mind. She was just sorry that it had to be that way.

"Well, that's between me and Wade. But I'm glad you approve," she told them.

The sun was starting to go down, and she thought about Wade, sitting alone in his tiny house, wishing for a home with her and their children. Dave had always thrown away the pictures they'd made him, but Wade had kept them safe.

Did she really need to know anything else about him?

Maybe he hadn't exactly said he loved her, but he'd constantly shown her with his patience, kindness, and even his dreams for the future. She hadn't told him she loved him, either, but that was about to change.

"Do you guys want to do something special for Wade?" Madison asked, looking down at the kids.

They all nodded. Madison quickly got them up off her lap and seated at the kitchen table where she had them draw him pictures. It was a risk, considering they just barely kissed, but Wade had risked so much more for her that she wanted to do something big to show him how much she loved him.

WADE TRIED CONCENTRATING on the crazy relationship book Allie had told him to read. He didn't know why he was still reading it, considering Madison hadn't given him much of a response to everything he'd told her. But he'd really thought that if he showed her just how much he was trying, then she would understand that while he wasn't perfect, he desperately loved her and would do anything for her happiness.

He closed the book and stretched. Outside his window, he could see lights bobbing in the distance. Flashlights. Who would be out at this hour?

When he opened the door, Madison stood there with her children. They were each holding a sign. D.J.'s said, "Will."

Faith's said, "You."

Madison's said, "Marry."

And little Hope, in Madison's arms, had a sign that said, "Us?"

Was he dreaming?

"What's all this about?" he asked.

"I think the words speak for themselves," Madison said. "But if you want me to say them, here goes. I love you. Yes, I was upset with you for going behind my back to find Dave, but the more I thought about it, the more I realized that you quickly owned up to what you did, and you apologized. I believe you were genuinely sorry for hurting me. You took responsibility for your actions, and even though I gave you no reason to believe I was going to forgive you, you still shared the deepest parts of your heart, knowing I could easily break it. That's what love is to me. Being vulnerable and trusting each other even when it's hard."

She gestured at the kids. "They saw a side of their father today that confirmed that he doesn't care about them as much as we all hoped he did. He made it clear that the only reason he'd come back was to get my signature on those papers, so he could get the money. I also found out that he hadn't just been lying to me, but also to my mother, and he's a big reason we've been estranged for so long. But we're working on that, and even though it wasn't your intended action, in a roundabout way, it's thanks to you. She came because of him, and even though it wasn't what anyone expected, it opened up her eyes to his lies, and now we're all free."

He soaked in her words, trying to understand what they meant. Sure, he knew what the words on the papers read, and he knew what she was saying, but he couldn't believe she was finally saying them to him. "You love me?"

Madison wrapped her arms around him. "Enough to ask you to marry us. I know, it's tradition for the guy to do the asking, but you've already laid out your heart for me, and I wanted to give you something just as big, so you knew it wasn't just your heart on the line, but mine as well."

He wrapped his arms around her, and as he did so, the kids hugged them both, surrounding him with more love than he could remember having in a long time.

He stood there for a moment, reveling in the fact that he was surrounded by so much love. "I love you, too," he said.

Then he heard a voice call out, "Well, are you going to marry her or not?"

Enid. Of course.

But before he could answer, Allie's voice rang out. "We know you're going to marry her, so could you kiss her?"

"How about you all show yourselves so I know exactly who I'm dealing with?" He answered back. A line of flashlights turned on, revealing Enid, Caroline, Hayden, Andrew, Layla, Allie, Cole, and Madison's mother.

"I should have known that every Bigby would show up for this," he said, grinning.

"Oh no," Madison's mother said. "There are a lot of others, even though they're not here. But I have faith we'll be seeing them all soon enough. I tried escaping them, but Bigby love is too strong to stay away from for too long."

Bigby love was strong. Something his mother recognized, even in dementia. And as he looked down on Madison's smiling face, he was grateful she'd bestowed that love on him.

"Yes, I'll marry you," he said, bending to kiss her.

He was pretty sure everyone clapped, but with such a lovely woman to distract him, he couldn't be certain.

EPILOGUE

ne year later

THE BIGBYS WERE PREPARING for the first annual Bigby family reunion. Reconciling with Madison and her mother had convinced Enid to bring all of her children together because, as she put it, life was too short to not be surrounded with your loving family. The rest of the family was due to arrive in the next few days, but today, the core that had been together for so long was gathering in preparation.

Actually, Madison was fairly certain that the reunion was because even though her grandmother should be happy that she was finally getting her dream come true—a house full of great grandbabies to hold—greedy little woman that she was, she wanted more. Madison just hoped that her other Bigby cousins were strong enough to resist.

But maybe, they'd see that love was too wonderful to even try resisting.

She smiled over at Wade, who was cuddling their three-week-old daughter, Laverne, or "Lovie" for short, because they couldn't have Faith and Hope without love. And, with his mother passing only a few short weeks after their wedding, they felt it was only fit to honor her.

"Give me a turn with that baby," Gram said, stomping over to Wade. "You're such a baby hog. The only time I see anyone besides you holding her is when Madison's feeding her. It's not fair."

Wade smiled down at his daughter. "No one ever told me how wonderful it was, holding a baby. No wonder you keep demanding them from everyone."

She hadn't known a man could fall so deeply in love with being a father. He'd been there with her through it all. When she couldn't get out of bed because of her morning sickness, he'd laid there with her, rubbing her back, telling her how much he loved her and how grateful he was for her having their baby. He got up with her for nighttime feedings, and so far, she hadn't changed a single diaper. She didn't know men were supposed to be such hands-on parents, but it was a special gift, sharing this time with him.

Wade looked up at Gram. "Don't you have some other baby to hold? Where are the others?"

Allie entered the garden, carrying her wailing daughter. "I know, I know. I'll feed you in a second."

She sighed as she collapsed into one of the chairs and began feeding the baby. "All Julia wants to do is eat. And she screams if you don't feed her right away."

Allie's mother, Mary, walked in carrying an overstuffed diaper bag. "You were just like her when you were a baby. I thought for sure you were going to be up as big as a linebacker when you grew up, but no. You just liked to eat."

Madison smiled at the look mother and daughter exchanged. Allie and her mother had not always had such an easy relationship, but she loved how they'd grown closer due to the birth of Allie's daughter.

Layla entered the garden, chatting with a pregnant woman near her own age as Andrew followed, carrying the baby carrier. Madison's heart was filled with joy as she saw Layla's closeness with her stepmother. Andrew planted a kiss on Layla's cheek, as he handed Layla their daughter. Gram dashed toward her. "I haven't held Estella in nearly two hours. Give her to me."

Layla laughed. "Not now. She has to eat."

Layla found a chair near Allie and started nursing her own baby. Gram turned and glared at Wade. "You see. It's not fair for you to not share with me. The other babies are busy."

Wade pressed a kiss on top of his daughter's head. "Caroline will be here soon. And since she's got two of them, she can't possibly need to feed them both at once."

Wade bent and whispered something in Lovie's ear.

Hope wandered over to her sister. "My turn to hold her," Hope demanded.

Wade looked up at Madison. "Why is everyone making me share? Maybe next time we need to have twins, triplets or something, so people will just leave me and my baby alone."

Madison's stomach hurt at the thought of having more than one baby. Even though Caroline's mom was there to help her, and Hayden also helped a lot, Caroline looked exhausted most of the time. As if on cue, Caroline entered the garden, pushing the twins in a stroller.

Of all the new babies, Caroline's made Madison's heart the happiest. After her miscarriage, she'd confessed that she'd been trying desperately to get pregnant, with no luck. And then it was as if someone had dumped fertility drugs in the water at Bigby Farm, because all the Bigby females ended up having babies within two months of each other.

Enid marched over to the stroller. "Which one doesn't need to eat?"

Caroline pointed at the one on the right. "Jessica just ate. But I think she just filled her diaper, so you'll have to change it."

Gram snatched the baby up. "Fine. I'll take a poopy diaper. I'm just glad one of you isn't being selfish with your babies."

Everyone laughed, and Gram whisked Jessica off to change her diaper. Caroline pulled Ashley out of the other side of the stroller, and joined the others in line feeding their babies. She smiled over at Madison. "I'm surprised you're not with us," she said. "It seems like that's all we do anymore. Sit around feeding babies."

Allie nodded. "At least you have two of them. I'm feeding as much as you are, and I've only got one."

Then she looked down at Julia and smiled. "But Mommy doesn't mind one bit."

Wade got up and handed the baby to Madison. "She's hungry too," he said. "I just didn't want to give her up."

Madison smiled as she gathered Lovie into her arms. She'd noticed her daughter fussing, but she wasn't going to take away Wade's joy. He took Hope by the hand. "Let's go see if we can find the others to play a game," he said, whisking her out of the garden.

Madison looked around at her family and smiled. Her mother would be flying in later today, and the rest of the Bigby relatives would be arriving over the next several days. But for now, it was just their small, but rapidly growing, group. Gram came back into the garden, cradling a freshly changed Jessica in one arm, and carrying a pitcher of iced tea in the other. "I was doing some reading, and you'll never guess what the leaves of the rutabaga will make."

The women all groaned in unison.

163

"My milk supply is just fine," Layla said. "I don't need one of your silly teas."

Gram grinned. "This isn't about your milk supply. This is about the fact that I need a baby great-grandson. What are you thinking, all having girls? It's like you're all conspiring to be the death of me. But don't you worry, I've got a plan."

Layla looked down at her baby, then back up at Gram. "It's too soon after having our babies for any of us to be thinking about getting pregnant again. We're not going to drink any of your weird concoctions that are supposed to enhance our fertility for boys. Go dump that stuff out, or I'm telling Andrew to take back the lavender ice cream he picked up at Lik's."

Gram looked at her in horror. "But Lavender Romance is my favorite."

"Dump it out," Layla said.

Wearing the cranky expression of a three-year-old who'd just been told no, Gram dumped out the pitcher over the side of the porch. "Well I'm not getting any younger, and I think you all need little boys. So hurry up and get to work."

They all laughed and shook their heads as Gram settled herself on one of the benches with little Jessica.

"Now," Gram began, turning all her attention to the baby. "I don't think the good Lord is going to let me live long enough to see your babies, but I pray that you will give your momma every bit as much of a hard time as she gave me about giving her grandbabies. Just you wait until she gets the grandbaby bug. She's going to want grandbabies so bad she can't stand it. And I want you to be firm in telling her no."

Gram bent and kissed the baby, then looked up at all of them. "If I can't get what I want, I'll have my revenge."

As the women finished feeding their babies, the guys all returned, carrying dishes of ice cream. And while everyone else got lavender, Wade handed Madison a bowl of vanilla.

"They may all love Lavender Romance," he told her. "But I'll be forever grateful for how much you make me appreciate vanilla."

As he bent to kiss her, D.J., Faith, and Hope entered the garden, laughing about whatever game they'd just played with Wade and the uncles. Maybe the Bigby family was all a little crazy, but Madison would be crazy to want anything else.

COMING NEXT IN ARCADIA VALLEY

http://arcadiavalleyromance.com/books/a-reservation-for-romance/

THE ARCADIA VALLEY ROMANCE SERIES

January 2017: *Romance Grows in Arcadia Valley*
February 2017: *Summer's Glory* by Mary Jane Hathaway
March 2017: *Muffins & Moonbeams* by Elizabeth Maddrey
April 2017: *Secrets of the Heart* by Lee Tobin McClain
May 2017: *Sprouts of Love* by Valerie Comer
June 2017: *The Thought of Romance* by Danica Favorite
July 2017: *On Board for Romance* by Annalisa Daughety
August 2017: *Autumn's Majesty* by Mary Jane Hathaway
September 2017: *Cookies & Candlelight* by Elizabeth Maddrey
October 2017: *Wise at Heart* by Lee Tobin McClain
November 2017: *Rooted in Love* by Valerie Comer
December 2017: *The Sound of Romance* by Danica Favorite
January 2018: *A Recipe for Romance* by Annalisa Daughety
February 2018: *Winter's Promises* by Mary Jane Hathaway
March 2018: *Donuts & Daydreams* by Elizabeth Maddrey
April 2018: *Joy of My Heart* by Lee Tobin McClain
May 2018: *Harvest of Love* by Valerie Comer
June 2018: *The Taste of Romance* by Danica Favorite
July 2018: *A Reservation for Romance* by Annalisa Daughety

ABOUT THE AUTHOR

A self-professed crazy chicken lady, Danica Favorite loves the adventure of living a creative life. She and her family recently moved in to their dream home in the mountains above Denver, Colorado. Danica loves to explore the depths of human nature and follow people on the journey to happily ever after. Though the journey is often bumpy, those bumps are what refine imperfect characters as they live the life God created them for. Oops, that just spoiled the ending of all of Danica's stories. Then again, getting there is all the fun.

Click here for a complete list of Danica's books.

Subscribe to Danica's newsletter for all her latest news: http://eepurl.com/7HCXj

You can connect with Danica on her website: http://www.danicafavorite.com/

On Amazon: https://www.amazon.com/Danica-Favorite/e/B00KRP0IFU

Or at any of the following places:

BB bookbub.com/authors/danica-favorite

twitter.com/danicafavorite

instagram.com/danicafavorite

facebook.com/DanicaFavoriteAuthor

READER LETTER

Dear Reader,

Wow! Can you believe that we are at the end of the Legacy of the Heart series? It's hard saying goodbye to our beloved Gram, Enid Bigby, after a novella and three books. But I think you'll agree that she, as well as her grandchildren, got the happily ever after that they so deserved.

I actually came up with Madison's story first, so writing this was both a joy and harder than I expected. Because she's been sitting with me for so long, I've been dying for her to find her happy ending. But I wasn't expecting it to be so hard to say goodbye.

You've probably figured out by now that I write a lot about following your dreams. For me, it's so important to encourage others in that pursuit, because I'm lucky enough to be living mine. I played with a variety of dreams in this series, because I want you all to know that whatever your dream is, it's important.

If you need a little encouragement in following your dreams, I've started a group on Facebook called <u>Your Story is</u>

<u>Valuable</u>. I'd love to have you join me in a safe place where you can share your dreams.

Or, if you're just a reader, I have a reader's group where you can join me and other people who love my books, and we can chat some more. <u>Danica Favorite Readers Group</u>

We all have a role to play in this world, and I know that God sees us as valuable, which is a message I hope you get from all of my books. Thanks so much for being on this journey with me!

Danica Favorite

ACKNOWLEDGMENTS

Writing this book came during a difficult season in my life, and I'm really grateful to all the friends and family who were there, supporting me while I worked like a crazy woman.

I want to thank the other Arcadia Valley authors for our time working together and for their contribution to this series. Also, thanks for promising not to kill off my beloved Enid. Enid lives forever!

JR Tague, thanks for being willing to take on this project to do my copyedits. Especially with the quick turnarounds and my insane schedule. And that fact that I kinda sorta forgot to hit send when I was supposed to, so I got it to you late. You're amazing to work with and I cannot begin to express my appreciation for you.

To my readers, thank you so much for taking the time to read my books and tell me how much they mean to you. I'm so grateful for you! If you loved this book, I'd love for you to leave a review, so others can share in the love.